ANDROMEDA, THE WOMAN HE LOVED, WOULD BE THE NEXT SACRIFICE TO THE MOST SAVAGE GOD OF ALL. . . .

"What about this Kraken, then? There must be some way to kill it."

Ammon laughed. "My boy, when the blood runs hot, memory runs short. You forget what happened to Argos." Nervous words were passed between the soldiers.

"The Kraken is the last of the Titans," Ammon continued. "Last of those great immortal beings who fought alongside Chronos against Zeus. It would take a god to kill it, and they say only Poseidon and Zeus among all the gods can control it. As for killing it, there is no way it can be done. No way known to man." Ammon shook a cautioning finger at the frustrated youth. "I believe in struggle, but not in needless sacrifice. If the entire city of Argos could not halt the actions of the Kraken, much less injure it, what can we hope to do?"

"Words will not save Andromeda. I will try to disable this monster by myself," declared Perseus. "I will not surrender the princess to save the injured pride of a fickle goddess!"

CLASH OF THE TITANS

Novelization by
Alan Dean Foster

From the Screenplay by
Beverley Cross

WARNER BOOKS

A Warner Communications Company

For my nephew David,
One to grow with. . . .

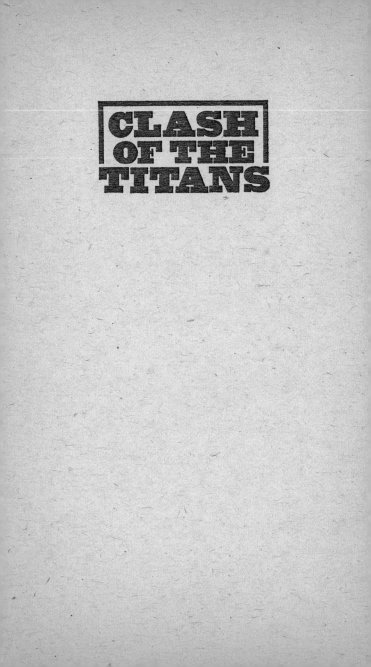

CLASH OF THE TITANS

It doesn't matter who sees it, or when.
It doesn't matter who hears it, or when.
It doesn't matter who touches it, or when.
The ocean is forever a constant
To gods as well as men.

—Old Greek Fisherman's Song

I

It is said among tellers of tales from Macedonia to Mesopotamia, from Crete to Carthage, that when the gods invented turquoise they set the finest of it down in Persia and dissolved the rest in the sea men call the Aegean.

Turquoise can be darkened by aging and by acids. That unfortunate morning it seemed the Aegean itself had been darkened by anger. Boreas and his daughters had stirred the seas into a rare tempest. Normally placid waters twisted with fury and foam assaulted the land as water warred in an endless battle with the shoreline for topographic supremacy.

Oblivious to the mighty conflicts of nature, tiny red crabs scuttled in and out of waves large enough to crush whole ships, searching for food. To them the eternal conflict involving ocean and cliff was as vague as the fogs which often caressed this particularly rugged coast. To them a towering wave was no more than a convenient servant, delivering a fresh coating of tiny food-things with each new, mighty roar.

While they did not fear the power of the waves, they hurried to scuttle aside the moment a more lethal force made its presence known. Racing sideways, they scrambled for favorite hiding places in the crevices and water-filled depressions eroded in the rocks.

One not quick enough was crushed to death. It was an idle execution, performed solely to amuse the perpetrator. Purpose, then, was the difference between man and wave.

The crab's death was an omen of sorts, but no oracle was needed to predict the intentions of that grim-faced line of armored figures making its way up the damp slope leading to the cliffs. They were bent upon murder more monstrous. Wind slapped at their eyes. Rain trickled down inside helmets and breastplates, warm and clammy.

A few of the figures sported beards. The curly hair was usually cut close to the cheeks and to a point at the chin. Cloaks did their best to keep rain from bodies. The enveloping material also served another purpose, for there were some among the line of marchers who felt misgivings about their task and were grateful for the concealment the cloaks provided.

Yet why should I worry, thought one of the dedicated soldiers? I only obey the orders of my king and priests. Was not this punishment we are carrying out decreed by them and approved by an offering to the gods? Did not the population of Argos cheer the decision, even hurling stones at the condemned along with the most vile insults? Why then, with such unanimity of support, should I be worried?

He stood a little taller, this soldier. His stride became more purposeful as he marched confident in the knowledge that the gods were with him and that he was Acting In The Right.

Besides, he was only a common soldier, and even if he disagreed with the decision of the priests, what could a mere soldier do against his king?

The column continued to snake its way toward the crest of the cliffs overlooking the turbulent sea. Its significance was marked by two things that were carried.

One was a large wooden chest much like an oversized coffin. The intended function, if not the design, was similar. Six soldiers balanced it on their shoulders.

The other was a small wailing bundle carried gently by a young woman. Occasionally her haggard face would dart to right or left, seeking freedom but finding only armor and sword. The infant in her arms moaned soft and steady, his complaints lost in the throatier wail of the wind.

Once the woman broke to her right and tried to flee down the damp rocks. Two soldiers caught her easily before she'd traveled but a few steps. She could not run very fast, burdened as she was by the child and sore, blistered feet.

No comment was made concerning the pitiful, aborted escape; not by the woman, not by the warriors guarding her. But they stayed closer to her now. The woman's face was wet and it was impossible to tell which tears fell from the sky, which from her eyes.

The soldiers backed off slightly as they reached the edge of the precipice. The woman cuddled the infant tightly in her arms, trying to shield it from the elements. Below the granite overhang lay the roiling Aegean. Spume flecked the rocks. A curious gull cried insultingly from above, fighting the wind to retain its seat in the sky.

A soldier who was more than a king but perhaps less than a man stepped to the edge of the drop He had no fear of falling. Tyrants are sometimes as ignorant of fear as they are of everything else. Acrisius of Argos was such a tyrant.

He turned back to the column, satisfied that no daring fishing boat waited beyond the rocks to haul in more than mackerel. The sea was clean of man.

He was a tall man, was Acrisius. Sharp of features and turbid of thought. His Corinthian-style helmet left only his eyes and beard visible. Its horsehair crest rustled in the wind.

"Get it over with," muttered one of the waiting soldiers, but so softly no one else heard. His was the only remaining uncertainty within the troop. They had not been selected because of any tendency to question, any more than they had for squeamishness.

Acrisius made a gesture. The two soldiers who flanked the woman grabbed her arms. They started to drag her toward the large wooden chest.

Until now fear and defiance had combined to hold the woman silent. When the soldiers finally took hold of her, what remained of her nerves finally gave way. She began screaming and trying to break free. It would have been impossible even if she had not been holding the child.

"Father, no! By all the gods, spare me, or at least spare the boy. He is blameless. Your own flesh and blood, Father!"

Acrisius's reply was low and thick with indignation. It cut through the howl of the wind.

"I am Acrisius of Argos, of the royal line of Argos. Among that line I acknowledge no bastards, nor the mother of one. I will not break with tradition to do that now." His gaze rose, traveled past her.

"I see here no flesh and blood of mine. Once I had a daughter. That is gone from me now. Did you not hear the verdict of the people? You have shamed the entire city. No easy task for one woman."

"Is love so great a crime that it must be wiped out with death?" she pleaded. The soldiers were lifting her still struggling form into the wooden chest.

He spat toward her, the spittle landing on the hem of her gown and mixing quickly with the rain. "Lust is not love."

"Would you know the difference well enough Father, to be the judge?"

He shook his head once, violent and signifying nothing. Again he made a sign to the soldiers. The cover on the wooden chest was carefully lowered into position and then bolted down From within came the muffled, now terrified screams of the child. They did not carry as far as Acrisius's heart.

He turned, raised his arms and declaimed to the storm.

"Bear witness, Great Zeus, and all you gods of High Olympus! I commit my daughter Danae and her bastard son Perseus to the sea. Her guilt and sin have brought shame to Argos. The people demand their justice, and I do my duty as their king. I, Acrisius the King, now purge her crime and restore my honor and the honor of the royal family.

"Her blood is not on my hands. It springs from her own actions and from the vileness that resided in her loins. From that moment she ceased to be Danae of Argos. From this moment she is no longer anything."

Lowering his arms, he stood silent for a moment, regarding the raging sea. Then he turned and signaled to the waiting soldiers.

"Now."

Six of them bent and lifted the heavy chest. They moved to the edge of the cliff. The chest had become unnervingly quiet, and the men were anxious to be rid of it. Swinging the container in gradually increasing arcs they finally launched it forward. It rose and hung for a moment in midair, a floating cradle of death.

Then it plunged downward to land with a violent splash in the foam. It bobbed to the surface where the waves began to toy with it. Soon it would smash to splinters on one of the jagged, spume-swept rocks below or be drawn beneath the surface.

Acrisius let out an indifferent grunt, glad to be rid of the distasteful business. As he turned to depart, one of his two officers put out a hand to stay him.

"My lord, should we not remain here a moment or two longer?"

"What for, Apulion? I have much work to do. There are tax rolls to inspect and appointments to be kept, and we have a new war to plan."

"I know that, my lord. But would it not be best to remain at least until we can be certain of the harlot's death?"

Acrisius looked back over his shoulder. A gust of wind shoved arrogantly at him, nearly making him lose his footing.

"That is as certain as the anger of the sea, and no death is more certain than that, Apulion." He grinned humorlessly. "If the chest does not sink or smash to bits on the rocks, then it will float out to sea. There, starvation will provide a slower and perhaps more deserved kind of death." He looked back across rocky slopes and distant fields toward cloud-masked Argos.

"I have spent long enough on this. I am only here because the priests suggested it would be a wise thing. Let us be back to the palace."

Apulion shrugged. "As my lord wishes."

Slowly the soldiers began the steady descent. Down slopes strewn with boulders, across cultivated lands, past clusters of farmers' huts and groves of olive trees. Beyond lay Argos the city: magnificent, rich, and decadent as the king who'd heaped wealth upon it through the conquest of others.

Swinging helplessly atop the waves, the chest bobbed and spun with each shift of the current. Lightning illuminated an unseen sky and accompanying thunder set both occupants of the wooden grave to sobbing. There was none to hear them save the single gull that hovered overhead, still battling the wind.

It was not unnatural for the gull to follow the path of the chest. Gulls soon learn that much of mankind's detritus holds edibles disdained and discarded by him, but quite suitable for the satisfaction of a gull.

This particular gull, however, was not interested in garbage. It continued to track the path of the chest as it skimmed the surface.

Or was it possibly the other way round?

The chest rode past the last granite tooth protruding through the surf. It slid out into the open sea, on a course that might carry it to Phoenicia or Aegypt or even lands more distant. The chest might survive such a journey. Its prisoners could not.

Soaring higher, the gull rose on unstable winds. Its wingbeats strengthened as it turned toward the islands that dotted the sea to the north.

Soon it had crossed the islands and was winging its way over other land. Northwest of fabled Corinth it flew, then high over Mount Parnassus. Untiringly it sped past Lamia and Dhomokos. It ascended to heights gulls usually avoid, and once it outraced a very astonished hawk.

A fisherman of special sensitivity looked up from his boat on the river Pinios as the gull passed overhead; he muttered a prayer to his favorite god. Shepherds near Elasson reacted not at all. They were familiar with such things because they lived in the very shadow of the mountain which reached from the Earth to the Heavens.

The gull's wings expanded as it charged straight for the center of the rumbling black nimbus which encircled the summit of the mountain It flew straight on, ignoring the lightning that crackled all around and the thunder which sent tremors through the solid stone of the peak and the hearts of men dwelling far, far below.

Palaces and temples constructed of pure white imagination began to materialize beyond the clouds. "Ghost marble" it was called by those who sometimes rashly tried to ascend the sacred mountain. Soaring structures resting firmly on foundations of deep belief and anchored in the subconscious of all men, these edifices were built partly on Earth, but mostly in the mind, where nothing is what it seems.

Nor was the gull. As it braked toward the most magnificent and sublime of all the palaces, the one which rode the uppermost crag of the mountain, its wings solidified and its body lengthened. When it finally touched down upon the dream marble, it was with feet set in thongs that pulsed a faint blue green.

They were the color of the sea and smelled faintly of its depths. So did their owner. Here above the friendly waves he was uncomfortable. This was not his dominion, but his presence was required.

The stocky, hirsute figure brushed angrily at his faintly glowing robes as the transformation concluded. He strode up familiar steps toward the Chamber of Assembly, frowning as he went. It is never easy to be the bearer of bad news, even if one is a god.

Thunder receded behind him as he entered the spacious room, its boundaries indiscernible. Mist that was composed not of water, but of the fog of eternity, drifted through the chamber. It obscured distance as this very place obscured time.

The not-fog reminded him pleasantly of favorite places within his own realm, and he relaxed a little as he strode the last few steps to the throne.

Flanking him within the room were figures that seemed motionless. They were not. It was just that they moved through an existence without boundaries or restrictions. As such, they were contemptuous of time.

There was Hera, he noted; always present when her husband sat on his throne. Aphrodite stood close by Athene, whose ever-present owl rode confidently on the goddess of wisdom's shoulder. Poseidon never cared much for owls. They sometimes preyed on the seabirds in his charge.

He shifted his path away from her and toward Thetis. The secondary sea goddess was currently whispering to Hephaestus. Poseidon did not begrudge her the intimacy. The god of fire and forge was the homeliest of all the gods and lame besides, not to mention the hardest working (if it can be said that a god may work hard). Poor Hephaestus was the least blessed of them all, his enormous strength notwithstanding.

Despite that, he always had a good word for everyone, god or mortal, and a better sense of humor than most. It would be wrong to call the lame god of fire human, yet it was true that of all the gods he was the most like the mortals who inhabited the Earth.

The throne was quite near now. Poseidon

could see his brother, brooding as usual atop the white dais. One hand tapped an arm of his seat while his chin rested on another hand, the great rippling beard meshing with the folds of his robe.

Zeus was the sea god's brother and though he ruled supreme, Poseidon alone among the assembled immortals did not fear him. Nor did he envy Zeus his responsibilities as ruler of Earth and Sky and ultimate arbiter of the gods' disputes and bickerings. No, Poseidon was quite content to be left alone in his watery kingdom. Excursions such as this one into the upper world made him nervous. The gods often created god-sized problems and troubles, and he preferred to remain amiably divorced from them.

But when Zeus called, even grumbling brothers were compelled to obey. That was part of the bargain they'd struck when under Zeus's leadership they'd overthrown Cronus and the Titans, and that was the agreement Poseidon now hewed to. So he'd gone where bidden, and watched, and returned now to damnably dry Olympus to make his report.

Zeus's stare turned from far horizons down to his approaching brother. Poseidon was struck by the other's haggard appearance. He did not look any older and could not, being immortal. But he could look tired.

"What news, my brother?"

The sea god executed a respectful half-bow. "It is done. As we feared might happen,

King Acrisius of Argos has abandoned his daughter and her child to the sea."

"And what of the people of the city and its priests?" Zeus asked, dangerously soft-spoken.

"They concurred fully in the decision. They would have gleefully stoned Danae to death and the infant with her, if Acrisius had not given them his own brand of justice, to keep blood from his hands and the streets of the city."

Thunder rumbled through the chamber and down the slopes of Olympus, the not-fog twisting uneasily at the violence. "Then he will be punished. All who concurred in this evil must be punished. A cruel and ruthless crime, a blasphemy!"

Tall figures clad in flowing robes and glowing vestments began to stir, turning to face the throne. There was about them all an air of the imperturbable, born from the knowledge that they need fear neither time nor death.

In his initial anger Zeus had half risen from the throne. Now he settled back. There was thunder in his expression as well as in the air.

"And he prays, oh so fervently, does this Acrisius, along with his perverted priests. Prays to *me* to forgive his savage jealousy and cowardly revenge. His incestuous desires thwarted, he would condemn to a lingering death even the daughter who still loves him." The great head shook slowly in anger and disbelief.

"And Argos joins with him in this monstrousness. She has *shamed* their honor." He snorted derisively.

" 'Their honor.' The honor of a city which supports a tyrant like Acrisius. Argos has grown fat and wealthy on the backs of others. Her gold is smelted with tears, her commerce supported by slaves taken in conquest from plundered cities."

Zeus may have been the most imposing figure in the chamber, but the most elegant and confident now crossed to stand calmly before the throne.

"Acrisius has always shown full devotion to the gods of Olympus, my husband." Hera toyed with her necklace, pretending to watch only the sparkle and flash of unearthly jewels in the mist-diffused light.

"Can you condemn a warrior simply for being successful? His people follow him willingly because he leads them to success after success. Those same conquests which have enriched Argos have paid for many a magnificent temple dedicated to you, great Zeus, father and ruler of the gods."

"A hundred such deeds cannot atone for one such callous murder. A thousand temples or sanctuaries, whether dedicated to me, or to you, Hera my wife, or to any of us,"—he made a sweeping gesture that encompassed the other immortals nearby—"cannot wipe out or forgive this one, contemptible act of blood."

Hera shrugged. "Is Acrisius then so much worse than many another worshiper, the actions of Argos any more vile than that of a dozen other warrior cities? Besides, what can it matter, the death of one girl and her child?"

"One girl . . . Danae was his own *daughter*! You know my feelings when the sanctity of the family is violated."

"Indeed I do," Hera murmured. Zeus eyed her uncertainly for a moment before his anger again overwhelmed all other thoughts.

"And this abomination was condoned— nay, approved—by the priests and the populace of Argos. They have lost all respect for themselves, and for the teachings of the gods, if they can allow such vileness."

"I cannot deny that many seemed pleased by the decision, brother," put in Poseidon.

"After a lifetime's respect and devotion," Hera murmured, "you would cast down a devoted worshiper?"

"Enough! I love you, Hera, but you twist words the way my brother Hades twists souls." He rose. "I have decided. Acrisius must be punished, and his heartless people along with him." He looked down at his impatient brother.

"Poseidon, I command you to return to your element. I command you to raise the wind and the sea. Destroy Argos! It shall be a lesson to those who would think of flaunting injustice and evil, in the name of serving the gods. I will

23

not allow my laws to be used to justify such murderous acts.

"To make certain that not one stone of the city remains standing, not one creature crawls free to mock my justice, I command you to let loose the last of the Titans. Let free the Kraken."

It takes much to upset a god, but the mention of that last survivor of the great war of an eternity ago sent a shudder through the room. Of all the gods, only Zeus and Poseidon had the will and strength to control one of the Titans.

Now only one of those titanic beings remained, safely caged and chained away to remind the gods of Zeus's ancient triumph. No greater punishment could be wreaked on man or god than to expose him to the wrath of that monster, who rested and waited for the rare occasion on which he might be allowed to vent a thousand years of frustrated fury.

"The kingdom of Acrisius must be destroyed."

"As you command." Poseidon bowed again, sorry for the work he now had to perform. Yet he could not go against his brother's decision. That was the Law.

"Stay a moment, Brother."

Poseidon paused, glanced back toward the throne. Already the anger was fading from Zeus's face, replaced now by an expression of concern as deeply felt as his often capricious fury. The sea god waited patiently. He knew his brother well enough to guess what was coming.

"Danae and her son have been cast by Acrisius into the care of the sea. Into your care," Zeus said softly.

"Make certain no harm befalls them. Speak to the waves and to all who dwell beneath. Make certain they convey mother and child safe to some remote and peaceful shore. Go now, and swiftly be about this business."

"By your command." Once more the sea god turned away. He strode out of the chamber, to be swallowed by the mists.

Zeus slowly descended from the throne. Hands clasped behind his back, he walked toward a distant, curving shape. Hera moved to stand close by Aphrodite and Thetis. The mist swirled tightly about them, trying to overhear their whispers.

"No pity. No mercy. I have seen him upset over such mortal triflings before, but never like this." Hera sounded concerned. "Why should this instance rouse him to such fury? There are more corrupt cities than Argos and worse tyrants than the dutiful Acrisius."

Thetis and Aphrodite exchanged a glance. Hera was usually understanding, but it was difficult to be sure.

It was the sea goddess who finally spoke. "His reasons are not entirely impartial. His involvement is personal, Hera. We had hoped to spare you such information."

Hera's gaze rose toward a higher heaven.

She sighed, said nothing, and waited expectantly. This was a revelation she had experienced all too many times before.

"Zeus loved the girl," said Aphrodite.

"This Danae?"

Thetis nodded. "She is rumored to be very beautiful. So beautiful that her father Acrisius grew jealous and kept her guarded from the eyes of men, locked behind iron doors. His own passions for her he refused to acknowledge, but he would let no other have her. She could not understand. Their frustration fed off each other's."

"Go on," said Hera, knowing what she would hear but as always, curious about the details. Her husband was famed and worshiped for many things, but marital fidelity had never been one of them.

Aphrodite continued when Thetis could not. She was not as reticent to discuss such matters, which after all fell within her province of administration.

"Zeus transformed himself into a glittering shower of gold and visited her. Visited her, and loved her as a mortal man. Father Zeus is notoriously persuasive at such times, and Danae, locked away for years, was understandably receptive to his sympathetic advances."

"Then why should I show any compassion?" wondered Hera. "Why should I care what happens now? Let her drown, and the child with her."

"But it answers your question, Hera," Thetis explained. "Do you not see the torment father Zeus is undergoing? The child Perseus is his half-mortal offspring, his son. That is why he must be saved. The threat to him is what prompted so extreme an outburst of hatred against Argos and its king. Perhaps Acrisius's crime and the consent of his people would have doomed the city anyway, but because of the child's heritage Argos's fate was sealed the moment her people voted to expose Danae and her son to the elements."

"See," murmured Aphrodite, pointing across the floor. "It begins."

Zeus had halted before a strange construct. It was a model of an amphitheater, a god-toy within which he could observe the playacting that men called their lives. With a touch here, a gesture there, the gods could alter the play, moving and shaping events from above. It amused Zeus to form his stage in the image of man's own.

Behind the shimmering metaphor were dark marbled walls filled with row on row of figures set in small niches. Those mortals whom the gods presently attended to were represented by such figures. Most men were not represented, their life-streams being of no importance to the future of the world. Occasionally a figure would be added, sometimes another would be removed. Empty niches awaited others destined to play important roles in the course of human history.

Two small statuettes stood motionless in

the center of the amphitheater, facing one another on the stage of life.

Zeus had placed them there earlier. Now he stood gazing thoughtfully down at them. Events could be altered, but not fate. How then had he managed to put himself in so difficult a position? It was not the first time. But there was nothing to do now but follow fate through.

One figure, stiff and stonelike, was a simulacrum of the tyrant of Argos; the other, a young woman cuddling an infant. Zeus shook his head dolefully. He did not enjoy such moments, but he was compelled to determine their resolution.

If only men would learn to emulate the teachings of the gods. Yet they persisted in acting like men. And what of the gods, he thought? Do we not sometimes lower ourselves to act like mortals? It was a disquieting thought for one who was not supposed to show doubt.

He lifted the statuette of Danae and the baby and set it carefully in an empty, waiting niche in the near wall. It was the still formless shape of the male infant which held his attention.

What kind of future had he unwittingly set that child on? What larger part might he play in the game of life?

Well, that was for the future, a bare moment from now. For the present ... he lifted the statuette of Acrisius.

Hades, my dark distant brother, make room in thy kingdom. Many immigrants are soon to arrive. As he thought, his fingers tightened slightly on the statuette. . . .

II

"My lord!" The soldier looked on with concern as King Acrisius suddenly bent over in pain, his arms wrapping around his chest. The little knot of warriors halted just inside the entrance to the palace.

"Nothing... it's nothing, Kimosos." Then he winced again, his eyes bulging wide in surprise as another sharp pain shot through his chest.

The soldier watched helplessly as the king's face twisted in agony. Then his gaze turned to look back toward the opening on the main square.

A troop of ten guarded the palace entrance. The guard was necessary for appearance, as well as for another less publicized purpose. For while most inhabitants of Argos thought Acrisius a brave and noble leader, there were those few fanatics who believed him a vicious tyrant worthy of assassination. The guard and the populace took delight in such attempts on the king's life, for it would mean another traitor to hang by the heels in the square, swinging until dead for the amusement of casual passersby.

The guard of ten—the most brutal and insensitive men in the royal phalanx—had stepped back into the shelter of the entryway and were muttering nervously to one another. Outside, the wind had risen with unnatural speed: it howled and shrieked and tore at the marble facing of the palace while citizens scurried for cover.

Acrisius's arms moved away from his chest and he took an unsteady step forward. Immediately his arms tightened again around his ribs and this time he stumbled to his knees howling with pain. He appeared suddenly incapable of speech, and unreason was rising in his eyes.

Terrified, his bodyguards dropped their weapons and fled in all directions.

"The vengeance of the gods!" yelled one who had mounted the cliffs that morning with uncertainty, but who had done nothing to stay the course of injustice.

"Come back!" shouted the officer Kimosos. "Come back, cowards! The decision was just. The people and the priests approved it, as did you yourselves." He waved his sword warningly at the retreating backs of the king's body-guards.

"It's only another storm, you fools! I will see you all set on the rocks with your guts ripped open for the birds to feed upon!" But threats did not slow the pace of those running from their king. They were swallowed up by the bowels of the palace, a refuge whose strength and solidity was suddenly vanishing.

Kimosos bent to his king. "My lord, I will have them tracked down and properly dealt with. You need stronger men for your personal guard. Men who are fit to match your own . . . your own . . ."

Kimosos stumbled away, the back of one hand covering his mouth, his shield clattering to the marble floor. He had looked into the king's eyes. In them he had seen madness, and his own incipient destruction.

Wind roared through the columned buildings, tore potted plants from atop balustrades and porticos, and ripped at the friezes worked by dying slaves to immortalize their uncaring masters. Dust filled the air. Oak and olive trees began to splinter under the force of the gale while smaller bushes were uprooted and thrown through the streets.

Men and women who had thought themselves the chosen stumbled about in confusion as they sought shelter from the anger of the sudden storm.

It blew straight in off the Gulf of Argolis

and from the Aegean beyond, that wind. It rose from the far stretches of the Mediterranean, nurtured by sources beyond the range of human perception.

Near the seaward side of the city, terrified soldiers fought to close the great harbor gates against the wind, as though they could shut out the storm like some mortal, but close by the water's edge the gale was too strong. The gates were thrown open, the soldiers sent tumbling like toys in the dirt.

The seas have their own private places. But man persists in searching them out, probing and peeking with his tiny devices to see what lies beyond the next overhang, beneath the next reef. There are some places never to be discovered and best left forever undisturbed.

Poseidon glided purposefully toward one such place. Ahead lay a massive underwater seamount fronted with metal worked by Hephaestus himself. Those gates, requiring a thousand mortal years to forge, had to be strong enough to hold something older than a god.

Bubbles larger than boats occasionally emerged from cracks between mountain and metal. They burst there in the dark depths or worked their buoyant way upward around unhealthy-looking sea growths: distorted corals, bloated anemones, hideous sponge things noisome with coatings of luminescent slime.

A rush of bubbles erupted from behind the massive doorway. The sea god knew the thing beyond sensed his coming. It hated him, as it hated all the gods who had destroyed its kin and taken mastery over the world. But Zeus had bound it, kept it alive for millennia, and it would do his bidding.

If it could not kill them, it would settle for killing whatever was offered.

The great bars on the doors were thick with crustacea and tangled growths, but even these odd life forms moved aside at the sea god's command. Even cleared, it required all Poseidon's inhuman strength to draw those bars aside. Among the gods only he and Zeus could master the creature, but even so, it was prudent not to challenge it unnecessarily.

It knew already what was expected, and moved impatiently inside its cage, eager to be about its task.

Poseidon slid the last bar aside, then moved away as he tugged the great doors open.

A head emerged hesitantly from the opening in the side of the seamount, a head larger than the entire figure of Poseidon. It was followed by an immense, dark body propelled by a huge scaled tail. The Kraken possessed a pair of arms and below them, a pair of cephalopodan tentacles lined with rasp-edged suckers.

It paused there a moment, enjoying its freedom. The horny crested skull turned right to left, the massive beak opening and closing.

"Go!" Poseidon finally ordered it, sickened

by the sight of the grotesque aberration. "Go and be quick with it, lest I shut you back in your hole now."

The Kraken did not speak, nor could its fixed face smile, but Poseidon sensed it was not impressed by his threat. It remained a moment like that, drifting in the water. Then it turned away, the eyes moving reluctantly downward. The ancient bonds Zeus had imposed on it remained unbreakable.

It kicked once with its enormous tail and was gone, racing to the surface. Poseidon watched it depart with a mixture of disgust and relief.

The fishermen were laughing as they related once again the story of Danae and her bastard, joking about what they might do if they happened to chance upon the floating burial chest. No need, they chuckled, to waste such a fabled beauty if they happened upon her. Once they were finished with her they could always replace her in the ark–chest. No one in Argos would know, or care.

The waters beneath them erupted. A head far larger than their ship shattered vile dreams and dreamers into small bits. The Kraken hung suspended a moment above the sea before all four massive limbs and its immense upper body fell with a thunderous crash back to the surface. It had not even noticed the small fishing craft.

A wall of water fifty feet high bulged upward and raced toward the harbor at the head of the narrow inlet. The soldiers on the walls saw the angry green cloud rushing at them through the windblown dust, but had no time to flee—only time enough for final, hasty prayers, and a scream.

Tons of water swept over the city gates, sending great blocks of granite flying like grains of sand. Marble pillars that seemed thick enough to support mountains snapped like broom straws.

People repented too late and to no avail. Waves threw them against stairways and walls or sent them spinning like dolls through the river channels that had once been broad avenues. A few refugees sought shelter in Argos's largest edifice, the royal palace. Smaller, more peaceful towns and cities had given up their gold and people to raise that wonderful structure. In isolated places its marble was still stained with their blood.

Now vast, tireless ocean swells swept around the columns and through the grand rooms. The altars of the various gods were swept aside along with the pitiful reminders of a lost dominance: swords and shields, coins and vases and stolen statuary.

Acrisius lay slumped still on the floor of the main hall, ignored by his people as they ran for shelter around him. The roaring outside grew louder. Water swirled around his feet, but he was unable to rise.

Then a peculiar groaning heralded the shattering of the roof. The falling stone slabs spared him long enough so that he had a single glimpse of the awful visage of the Kraken, towering above.

With that sight came the knowledge of the source of his sudden downfall. He cried out a curse against the gods who had chosen to punish him so; then he died, crushed like a beetle beneath a section of roof weighing half a ton. To the implacable, efficient Kraken, his was merely another corpse.

That night it seemed that evening came early to the Gulf of Argolis. A thick red sun oozed slowly into the western horizon, throwing vermilion across a scene of desolation. Within the once proud city, nothing moved. Not a horse, a dog, a rat.

From nearby Navplion and Mikinai travelers arrived to view the destruction. They made large offerings for many nights thereafter to appease the anger of those they knew to be responsible for Argos's fate, lest it later lap over to consume them as well. And there was less talk in the cities bordering the gulf of taking up the mantle of conquest that had so enriched the great city.

Zeus opened his hand and blew the dust that had been Acrisius to the four winds. In his mind he saw the Kraken reluctantly return to its abyssal lair, once more to be shut in by Poseidon.

It was done.

Somewhere far below and away, far from ravaged Argos, a battered and seaworn wooden chest drifted on a calm evening sea.

Eventually it grounded gently on a white sand beach. No storm raged here, no howling wind or monstrous shape of vengeance. A small boat, skillfully guided, could not have made a better landing. For a moment, nothing could be heard save the soft lullabies of wind and surf. Then the cry of a waking child rose above the lap of the advancing tide.

Damp with the smell of his recently visited kingdom, Poseidon stood once again in the home of the gods. His expression was grim and it was clear to his fellow immortals that he wished to be elsewhere.

"It is finished," he told the figure standing next to the flickering silhouette of the amphitheater. "Argos is punished and Danae and her child have been carried safely to the island of Seriphos."

Zeus nodded approvingly. "A good choice."

"I did not choose it," Poseidon muttered, distressed by the whole business. "The waves chose it. They have mind and will and direction of their own."

"Nevertheless, it is a good place; its people kind and better than most men. It will serve. There let Danae and her child live safe and happy."

"And what of Argos?" Hera asked bitterly.

"What of its history and those who once faithfully worshiped the gods?"

"Its history is one of murder and pillage and is best forgotten," Zeus replied angrily. "Let the men who live near its site look upon it from time to time and remember the wrath of the gods. Let them know that worship does not excuse evil. I want no such worshipers as lived in that accursed city. Let it thus remain."

"For how long?"

" 'How long'?" For the first time in a while, Zeus smiled. "You speak like a mortal, wife. What is time to us? It can be whatever we wish. A mortal day, no more here than the wink of an eye. Twenty years, one night of love. Time is the human tragedy. But to us it has no more meaning than shape, which we can alter at will and whim. I am surprised to hear you speak of it, Hera.

"Aphrodite's beauty need never fade. Your hair need never turn to gray. But poor earthly man is in the grip of age the instant he is born. In the end he passes into the grim lands of the dead and the rule of my brother Hades and he is forgotten—nothing more than a shadow in a dream. I feel for poor man, trapped by the memory of Cronus."

"At least he knows his destiny," Hera countered. "His boundaries are finite."

"Would you then trade yours for his, sweet Hera?" Zeus chided her gently. "Would you abandon immortality?"

"No. But sometimes I wish I had mankind's certainty."

"About what? About death?"

"No. About purpose. Man always seems to have purpose. We have only time." She eyed him sharply, challengingly. "Tell me, great ruler of Olympus: what lies waiting for the gods at the end of time?"

He looked away uncomfortably. "Mother of women, I like not your questions. There is no end for the gods. We are immortal and eternal."

"You believe that," she replied. "I believe that. But does man?"

"Who cares what man believes?" Thetis looked disapprovingly at her friend. "You worry too much, Hera."

The queen of the gods shrugged, looking very human. "It's my nature to worry, Thetis. One of us must."

Nothing more was said. Their attention turned back to the amphitheater of life. The first act had come to an end. Would there be more, or was the play short and already finished? Time meant nothing to them and did not pass as man knows it to, but down on Earth it was otherwise. Those crowded around the symbolic amphitheater watched with considerable interest to see what might happen now.

Even a god can get bored.

No matter what the gods thought of it, the passage of life was still called time by men. It turned its steady pirouette, setting the pace of the world. Cities rose and fell, great works of art were created and lost. All these things and more marked the passage of time in Hellas.

Children rose from infancy to adulthood. Those in Athens or Corinth, in Sparta and the other great cities of the Peloponnesus became schooled in the ways of statesmanship or literature, sculpture or commerce. They were being groomed to become leaders of men.

On a small island another child was blossoming. His library was the sea; his study, the many manifestations of a bountiful nature; and his mentors, the simple, pastoral people of the isle known as Seriphos.

From his mother he learned much of statesmanship and of how falsehoods can raise a massive city on shaky foundations. He learned that power supported by corruption is doomed to collapse, and that morality is the difference between strength and tyranny. Surprisingly, from her he also learned compassion.

He grew up with little knowledge of fear, living closely with the most violent storms the Aegean could raise. He swam like a dolphin and ran like the horses he mastered at an extraordinarily young age.

Once he broke both legs attempting to fly after a thieving gull. More than the pain, there was simple astonishment at failure, for having so successfully emulated runners and swimmers, he had thought flight simply another skill to master.

The people of Seriphos, who had taken in the castaways many years earlier, took personal pride in his progress. He had a whole village of mothers and fathers. The island children, who instinctively knew themselves to be less than he, played freely and delightedly with him, for he was open and guileless and free of pride. He was a friend to everyone and everyone was his friend, but for all that he held no false illusions about the nature of man. His mother's instruction was too thorough for him to grow up innocent of evil and duplicity.

On an island of fishermen it was only natural that when grown he too would practice the skill of coaxing from the sea its finny bounty. He often went out alone, to return with catches twice the size of those brought in by well-crewed, much larger craft.

Still, the islanders did not envy him, for he shared much of his catch with those whose luck had been bad, and so he was praised for his generosity as much as he was admired for his skill. It was even whispered by some that he was a favorite of Poseidon, that the sea god assured the boy of a good haul every time his boat set out.

That was not the case, however. It was simply that the boy was a good fisherman.

He lay down on the deck of the boat, his eyes closed against the glare of the summer sun. With only a loincloth on his body browned by Apollo's radiance, he was as lean and muscular as the traveling dancers who sometimes visited the island. His hair was thick and curly, dark as the sea on a moonless night. It was a man's body now, though the face still held some of the joy and freshness of adolescence.

Sweat rolled hotly from his sides and he used an arm to shield his face from the sun. Soon he would have to rise to pull in the net. The salty aroma of seaweed and fish rose from the small hold, already half full of blue-scaled captives.

He squinted at the sun. For an instant, he had the strange sense of staring into a face—the face of an old man with a thick white beard. But the face quickly vanished, it was only the sweat stinging his eyes.

He sighed, thinking of the cool wine he would drink in the taverna when he had disposed of the day's catch. He did not know that that small pleasure would elude him tonight. He did not know that his destiny was near.

His name was Perseus.

Zeus held the statue of the lithe young man in one hand, eyeing it without expression. He felt oddly ill at ease, as he often did when important events were about to unfold—events which sometimes even he, king of the gods, could not control. It was an awkward sensation for one with an eternity of accomplishment behind him.

Everything had gone so well, but he was still bound to act only within his own laws; and something seemed to be threatening them now, perhaps threatening even his very rule.

Then again, it might only be his stomach, which was subject to depressingly humanlike convulsions from time to time. Such discomforts were only indications of internal upset, not harbingers of the future.

A little less ambrosia next time, he told himself firmly. You're not the god you used to be.

His awareness of presence was as keen as ever, though. He turned to see Hera walking toward him, accompanied by Thetis, Aphrodite and Athene. It was good to see Athene with them. She was his favorite child and always supportive of his actions, though she from time to time displayed a disconcerting tendency to act on her own initiative.

He wished for Poseidon's gruff council, but his brother preferred the ocean depths to the rarefied coolness of Olympus. Oftentimes he envied his brothers their limited, special domains, even that of dark Hades. Their problems seemed simple, their eternities uncomplicated.

But someone had to rule, and he had taken the responsibilities upon himself. He smiled slightly, trying to imagine Poseidon coping with sweet Hera's intricate plots.

"Greetings, Father Zeus," said Athene brightly.

Ah, sweet daughter and fount of wisdom, Zeus thought. How I would like to set aside the mantle of ruler for a while, to be free of these devious dealings and decisions. You alone understand the reasons for my occasional sojourns down to earth to live and love among the mortals. Goddess of wisdom, you would make a fine ruler.

But he knew that could not be. The mantle of ruler was fixed. He would have to carry it, no matter how it tired him, until the end of time.

Hera was staring at the statuette her husband still held.

"Perseus," he told her. "Grown to a young man. Honest and caring, athletic and intelligent despite his lack of a formal education."

"Handsome, too." Aphrodite eyed the statuette appraisingly, her lips pursed.

Zeus glared at her warningly. "None of your games, now. The boy is uncomplicated. Save your wiles for more experienced mortals."

"But Father Zeus, surely a little innocent divine inspiration could but help speed the boy's maturation."

"You'll mature him beyond his time, and he doesn't need that. Stay away from him."

"Oh, very well." She crossed her arms and looked piqued.

Aphrodite's interest only annoyed Hera. "Since you've taken such an interest in his life, what do you plan to do with him now that he's become a man?"

"I have done enough," Zeus said, sounding quite pleased. "He has enjoyed a happy childhood, something which escapes most men. He has the advantages of a strong body, a handsome face, and a sharp mind. What more could I give any mortal, what more could one desire or deserve? Now he is a young man. The rest must be left to him . . . and to chance."

"Since when did you ever leave anything to chance?" Hera murmured, but too softly for anyone to hear.

"We are not here to discuss the future of this boy," said Thetis, "but that of my mortal son, Calibos." Her tone was stiff and anxious. "That is why we were summoned."

"Yes," Zeus agreed, placing the figure of Perseus carefully in its niche in the wall and choosing another from the endless rows. "That is a future that cannot be left to chance." His expression changed abruptly, darkening like one of the storms he so often raised over the Earth.

"His crimes are unforgiveable. They are too many and too monstrous to be ignored any longer. I have overlooked them, allowed them to pass unnoticed until now, but I can no longer continue. To do so would make the laws of the gods less than a mockery among men. This cannot be permitted. We must abide by the laws set down amongst us and so must our minions on mortal Earth."

"Be merciful to him! Show pity, I beg of you."

"Do not beg me, Thetis." Zeus eyed her distastefully. "It is unbecoming for a god to beg, even of another god. I have said that I have overlooked the crimes of this Calibos again and again. I cannot do so any longer. He has exhausted my patience and spat on my charity."

"One more time," she pleaded desperately.

"Impossible!" He waved angrily and thunder echoed through the halls of Olympus. "Calibos has had every advantage a mortal could ask for. As patron goddess of the wealthy city of Joppa you have spoiled and indulged him since birth, Thetis. Perhaps that is part of the trouble. Mortals seem to turn out better when compelled to earn their fame and wealth.

"You gave him the Wells of the Moon near Joppa to rule. No lusher place existed on Earth, and what has he done with this gift? Hunted down and destroyed every living creature of beauty for sport and personal pleasure."

"He has always been high-strung."

"That hardly excuses turning a paradise into a wilderness. He even dared to trap and kill the sacred herd of flying horses who dwelt there. For their meat!" The massive head shook slowly in disbelief. "One of the wonders of the Earth, obliterated to sate the palate of a single perverse gourmand, for such is what Calibos fancies himself. He left only the stallion Pegasus; because of him the race of men will not know the beauty nor have the services of the race of flying horses.

"Well, my dear Thetis, he has fancied himself too much. He thinks himself handsome and intelligent as a god. Even if it were not for his other repulsive crimes, this blasphemous assumption alone would be sufficient to damn him.

"It is for this and many other obscenities that he must be punished."

"No . . . be merciful, Father Zeus. Do not kill him."

"I do not intend to kill him, but not out of mercy. His noisome habits and likes disfigure his mind and thoughts. So then I command that his form be changed to reflect his thoughts. He shall become abhorrent to human sight."

Carefully he set the statuette of Calibos on the floor of the amphitheater of life.

Zeus glared at it, his eyes glowing as he pronounced his verdict. "He will be shunned by all, forced to live as an outcast in swamps and vile places. No longer master of the Wells of the Moon he shall henceforth be Lord of the Marshes. He will be transformed into a mockery of man. Let his own cruelty be mirrored by his appearance. Let him appear as his own thoughts reveal him to be!"

A different thunder rumbled around them. The figurine shimmered and shifted, its outline contorting beneath a baleful light. What finally coalesced might once have been a man. Now it sported a horribly deformed face topped with horns, a lizard's tail, one cloven foot: the reptilian part of Calibos's nature had flowed out of his mind to wash over and alter his body.

"This is my judgment." Zeus turned away from the amphitheater to place the distorted figure of Calibos back into its niche.

Thetis gazed down at the floor, unable to look any longer at the deformed statuette. She knew full well Calibos's crimes and sins, but if he was guilty, then at least some of the fault was her own.

Nevertheless, she knew he was not, could not be wholly evil. If he was damned, it was by being part mortal. She would not abandon her son, not even at the risk of facing Zeus's wrath.

"I implore you to reconsider, Father Zeus. Calibos was to marry the Princess Andromeda, heiress to Queen Cassiopeia of Joppa. He would rule all Joppa and Phoenicia."

"I will not stand in the way of an honest marriage," said Zeus formally. "Let the princess look on him now, as he truly is. Let her see his thoughts reflected in his face. If she still desires to marry him, then let it be so." He smiled thinly.

Turning away from them, he strode implacable from the sanctuary.

Hera moved to comfort the distraught Thetis, putting a reassuring hand on the sea goddess's arm. "Be comforted, my dear." She looked after her departing husband. "He can be as unpredictable as he can be vengeful. He may yet change his mind and give Calibos back his former shape."

"Never." Thetis's anger was subdued but no less deep than that of Zeus. "Had it been his *own* mortal child Perseus, he would have forgiven him. But for my son Calibos he has neither mercy nor hope."

"Be careful, my dear." Hera looked at her hard. "You cannot go against his will. That is the law. There is no connection between the life of Perseus and that of your offspring."

"Is there not?" Thetis became thoughtful. "Examples have a way of affecting decisions. Perhaps . . . oh, don't look so alarmed, good Hera. I would not *dare* to oppose the will of Father Zeus. I know I cannot help Calibos. But I have not been forbidden certain other actions."

"What 'other actions'? No, don't tell me. As you say, you cannot help Calibos. So there will be no marriage then to the Princess Andromeda for your son?"

"How can there be . . . now? Yet, if my son is not to have her, then no man will! There has been no talk of the woman in this, only of Perseus and Calibos.

"My priests in Joppa are loyal and responsive to their goddess. I will speak to them in dreams and omens. As my Calibos suffers, so will this Andromeda. I promise you."

"You should not kill her."

"Kill? Who speaks of killing? Not Father Zeus, and not I. I will not touch her. But it may be that, given time, even Calibos as he now appears will seem a better and better match to her. Zeus has said he would not oppose an 'honest' marriage between them. Perhaps 'events can be managed to induce such a seemingly unlikely joining to take place."

Hera smiled approvingly at the sea goddess. "I can see that my husband is not the only master of deviousness on high Olympus."

Thetis was not looking at her. "The law must not be broken," she was muttering, "but it can be avoided."

The catch had been good. Perseus felt the strain in his shoulders and biceps as he fought his way back to the beach. Dripping, he stood on the sand and glanced around for a second to orient himself. The glow of the driftwood fire was off to his right. He thought he'd emerged directly in front of it, but the ways of the currents could be capricious. He smiled to himself at his mistake and jogged toward the friendly light.

The night was warm, but the fire still felt good after the refreshing swim. Mossolion would distribute the surplus catch to those villagers who needed food. It was a task Perseus did not mind passing on to another. After all, it hardly mattered who received praise for distributing the fish as long as the fish went to those who needed it.

The moisture warmed away, he lay down on the sand next to the fire and studied the stars through the olive branches overhead. There was great Orion preparing to battle Taurus. There was the scorpion, and far away the others who'd been chosen to serve Zeus as beacons in the heavens. They were pleasant companions to have on a comfortable night.

He sighed, stretching luxuriously on the sand, and closed his eyes.

Thetis stared down at the perfect, limber shape of the young mortal and thought angrily of the punishment Zeus had inflicted on her own son. There was little she could do. But Zeus had said that Perseus's future was now in the hands of chance. Why should she not give chance a helping hand?

She refocused her gaze. The sanctuary was deserted, the amphitheater of life empty and glistening in the Olympian night. Moving furtively, she edged close to the structure. Her powers were but a pale fraction of Zeus's, but there was the amphitheater. Could it be different from another?

She knew of another amphitheater, one fashioned by men and not gods. What is one amphitheater to another but a chance of location?

She reached into the wall and chose the statuette of Perseus. She could not break it; that would truly bring the anger of Zeus down upon her. But she could place it somewhere else, unharmed.

The figurine could neither respond nor hear her as she spoke to it. "The son of Zeus is to be left to the whims of chance while mine is punished with deformity and disgrace. It is time for chance to make itself felt.

"You shall see something of the real world,

Perseus. It is rather different from Seriphos. It is time you came face-to-face with fear instead of fish; time to know the terrors of the dark and to look on death, as other mortals must do; time your eyes were opened.

"Reality, yes. I know something of reality, Perseus. It does not lie on the idyllic isle of Seriphos. It lies far to the east, across the sea. In Joppa, in the kingdom of Phoenicia. See then what you can make of yourself in reality, Perseus, and not in your little paradise! See if you fare as well there as my son!"

Checking one final time to make sure she was alone, she set the statuette down on the floor of the amphitheater. What indeed is the difference between one such structure and another? They are all settings for plays, stages to be performed upon.

The play's the thing, she thought with satisfaction. I have merely moved it to another stage.

Her fingers freed the figurine. . . .

III

Perseus stirred uneasily in his sleep. Something was different. The rich smell of the sea had faded and the crackle of the olive-wood fire no longer sounded in his ears.

Of course, the untended blaze might have sputtered out. He ought to make sure, for though the night was still warm he could take a chill. It had definitely grown cooler since he'd lain down.

He opened his eyes, and sat up quickly. Utterly bewildered, he gazed around at what shouldn't have been.

Row on row of white stone benches rose in a vast semicircle around him. They were overgrown with weeds and the beginnings of bushes. Only the moon and constellations overhead were unchanged, though the branches of the old olive tree no longer framed the stars.

The fire was not simply out: it had vanished completely. So had the sea and its sad song. In their place came the plaintive chirps of crickets and the occasional croak of a bullfrog. They were far more at home than he.

He rose and turned in a slow, baffled circle. The amphitheater was deserted. Underfoot the old stone paving was cracked and filthy with dust. Columns and arches were broken and evidenced signs of long neglect. Decorative statues still stood, but many were missing arms or heads. Clearly it had been some time since any plays had been staged here.

Perseus knew what the place was from stories told to him by the more worldly citizens of Seriphos, those who had traveled to other parts of the world. But he had never expected to see one. Certainly it seemed more appropriate as a background for a nightmare.

Something stung his left arm and he slapped at it. The slap felt as real as the bite, and the crushed, bloated smudge that had been a mosquito looked very familiar. If this was a nightmare, it was replete with an extraordinary amount of detail.

It didn't make any sense, this place. The philosophers sometimes said the same thing about life. He decided it was not a nightmare, for all that he might wish it was.

"WHO ARE YOU?"

Perseus whirled, but could not locate the source of the booming challenge. Echoing off walls and seats, it seemed to rise from all around him. He was too astonished to be afraid.

Again the demand: "WHO *ARE* YOU?"

The fishermen of Seriphos had told Perseus that when faced by a marauding shark, it was acceptable to feel fear, but most important not to show it. So he cupped his hands to his mouth and yelled back as bravely as he could.

"Show yourself first!"

"WHO ARE YOU?"

"First tell me where I am. Where is this place? Or at least tell me whoever or whatever you are."

"WHERE?" Forsaking its former challenging tone, the mysterious voice was now plainly as astonished as Perseus.

"Yes, where. Where am I?"

By way of reply several torches flickered into sudden, dancing life. From the shadows masking the primary stage entrance a bizarre figure abruptly appeared. It was clad in a splendid costume and richly woven cloak. In front of its face it carried a classical tragic mask topped by a tall false crown and fringed with golden whiskers.

The figure walked steadily toward Perseus, with all the dignity of a god . . . or a fine actor. Perseus could not tell whether the figure behind the mask and voluminous robes was male or female. But while that did not matter to him, he sincerely hoped the figure would turn out to be human.

The source of the powerful voice which

had challenged him was also evident, in the form of a twisted speaking trumpet made of metal. It was a bit dented and looked well used. Perseus relaxed just a little: demons were notoriously skillful smiths.

The approach soon degenerated into a half-march, half-shuffle, further hinting at the mortality of the figure. Soon it became evident the figure was walking with some difficulty. It then dropped all pretense at dignified posture and came to an awkward halt.

"WHAT DO YOU mean... MEAN?" There were some muffled sounds that might have been concealed cursing as the figure inspected the speaking trumpet and then set it aside.

When it spoke again, it was in a crusty, normal, and slightly irritated voice: "What do you mean, boy? You say you don't know where you are?"

Perseus shivered, beginning to feel the chill of the night as well as forces he did not understand. "That's right, I don't. I must have fallen asleep under the olive tree. Then I woke up here. Wherever 'here' is."

"That makes no sense." The apparition let out a groan of exasperation. "Curse this fool facade!" The figure struggled with the bulky mask, lifted it off and set it aside.

Its wearer stood revealed, an elderly gentleman of slight stature with no demonic pretensions. He was bearded and gray as the back of an old dog, but the eyes were still as blue as the Aegean with sparkle enough to match the light that sometimes bounced off the waves of that gentle sea.

He shuffled closer, inspecting Perseus with interest. The boy was an intriguing curiosity. If he was telling the truth, then his manner of, and reason for, being so peculiarly set down here promised nothing if not a subject for entertaining speculation.

"Now then, lad, where did you say you . . . no." Stroking his beard, he studied Perseus as a scholar might the pages of a rare book. "Let us be patient for a moment."

"But I am being patient, sir."

"Not you, not you," said the oldster, waving a hand irritably. "Me. My desires tend to race ahead of my thoughts. Especially these days." He chuckled. "Though it was often the same when I was your age, but the desires were different then.

"Now, never mind about this olive tree you say you were sleeping under. First we must exchange some necessary preliminary details."

"Whatever you think best, good sir."

" 'Good sir' . . . I like that. Now, I will explain first. My name is Ammon." He smiled and bowed slightly. "I am a poet and a playwright. I write comedies, which some sneer at as banal populist entertainment but which is a truer reflection of man and life than those endless, moaning tragedies. Though if you read carefully through all of the—"

"Excuse me . . . sir? Ammon?"

"Oh! Sorry, boy. My mind has a regrettable tendency to wander."

"I am called Perseus. I am heir to the ruined kingdom of Argos but have lived all my adult life on the island of Seriphos."

"Seriphos!" The old poet frowned uncertainly at the tall young stranger. "By all the gods, then how did you get *here*?" He looked Perseus up and down.

"It's evident enough you haven't just stepped off a ship. And I would have seen you approach the theater. Yet you're hardly dressed for a journey of such length. In fact, you're hardly dressed at all. How was this miracle managed, my boy?"

"I don't know." Perseus spread his hands in a gesture of helplessness. "I'm still not sure where 'here' is, remember."

"Your pardon. I forgot my own admonition, so overwhelmed am I by amazement. 'Here' is a long way from your Seriphos. This is the old amphitheater of the city of Joppa."

"Where?" Perseus sounded confused, though not embarrassed. "I confess I know little of the geography of the world, Ammon."

"The great trading city of Joppa," Ammon explained, "is part of the kingdom of Phoenicia. Surely you know of Phoenicia? You do not have the aspect of an idiot."

"Phoenicia! Yes, I know of that . . . of this land." He gazed again at the unkempt arena. "But how? Phoenicia lies many days by ship across the seas from Seriphos. I have not been on any ship. I was lying by the seashore, warming myself to sleep by a fire, studying the moon."

Ammon brightened. "Ah, the moon! That might well explain things. Moon affects the mind, you know. Well-known medical fact. Perhaps we'll think more clearly inside, out of its influence." He reached for the youngster's arm.

Perseus pulled away. "I'm not crazy, old man."

"Of course you're not," Ammon agreed. He threw a conspiratorial glance skyward. "It's just that eyes which can see the surface of the earth can't always perceive as clearly beneath rock and stone. If you follow me."

"I'm afraid I don't, sir."

"No matter. Just follow me."

This time Perseus didn't resist. Ammon led him through a series of once-grand arches whose delicate friezes were beginning to flake away. A magnificent charioteer with no head drove horses possessing fewer than the requisite number of legs. The reliefs were of plaster rather than marble, but to see such workmanship fallen into disrepair was enough to make an outsider wonder at the future of Hellenic art.

Past the arches appeared a stone staircase that led down below ground level. Ammon took up one of the spitting torches and continued downward.

"I apologize for all this dramatic finery

and the theatrical effects I was compelled to greet you with," the poet explained. "I am forced to utilize them now and then to frighten away the curious. Thieves would gladly carry off what little I have been able to preserve of the theater, though there is not much left of real value. Not much to them—priceless to me.

"I'm an old man and it's how I protect myself. Trumpets and masks. Besides, I always fought better with words than sword." He chuckled at his own humor.

"They think the amphitheater is haunted, that human sewage. And they're right. Though a writer first, I'm not such a bad actor. I've become very proficient at doing spirits and ghosts, for example."

"I can attest to that." Perseus grinned down at him. Then his attention was drawn to the weeds and roots poking busy green heads through cracks in the masonry.

"Why is everything so neglected? This looks to have been a fine theater once."

"So it was, my boy, so it was." Ammon let out a discouraged sigh. "The finest theater in Phoenicia, I dare say. But its current state is a sign of the times. The whole kingdom lives under a curse and the populace lingers always on the edge of despair. The people walk around muttering, 'call no man happy who is not dead.'"

"Did you write that?"

Ammon gave him a reproving look. "Hades, no. Though it's actually not such a bad line. But terribly pessimistic. I write comedies, remember? I am an optimist, though I know better. But I can't help it—an endemic condition. Anemic, my colleagues would say. I'm probably the last optimist in Joppa." He shook his head sadly.

"They all think of a half cup of wine as half empty. I think of it as half full. There you have the difference between optimist and pessimist, my boy."

"If you say you know better, then why do you remain an optimist?"

"Because it's nicer. They all say I'm mad, though." He burst into a raucous cackle that echoed off the walls as they started down a flight of rotting steps.

Perseus saw that the rock was dry and knew they were not close to a river or the sea. Like any good fisherman he'd developed an outstanding sense of direction. He decided they were now somewhere beneath the facade leading out onto the amphitheater stage.

Soon torchlight revealed the precious relics Ammon guarded so devotedly. There were devices for raising and lowering painted scenery, collections of masks and armories of fake weapons. Chariot fronts leaned uncomfortably against thrones, and costumes lay heaped in open chests. There were mounds of paint crucibles and the chamber was thick with the must of old makeup.

A lean, carnivorous shape slipped wraith-like from beneath a broken-legged couch, skittered across the floor like a great black cockroach. It was an old cat, skinny and tough and still full of fight. Much like its master, Perseus thought.

"Make yourself comfortable," Ammon said as he dug through a mass of papyrus scrolls. There was ink on a table nearby. From the size of the pile Perseus knew the poet to be prolific if not famous.

"If you can, that is," the old man added. "A cup of wine, perhaps? Half *full*." Again the wizened grin. "And I'll see if the cats have left us anything to eat. There was a chicken here earlier, cleaner than most. But my feline friends have the same affection I do for that noble fowl, and they are no less greedy." He turned away from the mass of writings and busied himself at a cabinet. Plates and other utensils clattered noisily as they tumbled from shelf to floor.

"Now then, my young friend, you truly claim to be Perseus, heir to the unfortunate kingdom of Argos?"

"Yes. Up to now I have lived in Seriphos." Pride filled his voice. "But some day I will return and reclaim Argos. You see, after I was born my mother and I—"

Ammon interrupted him with a casual wave. "Oh, I know about all that. Save your breath. Though I admit it is fascinating to meet one of the participants in so famous a tale. Yes, I know your history, my boy."

"You do?"

Ammon returned to the table with cups of wine, a clay amphora, olives, and a few fragments of chicken.

"Certainly." The poet looked roofward as he recited. "The beautiful princess. The jealous, demented tyrant. You and your mother thrown into the sea, the judgment of the priests and the people. The subsequent destruction of the city. Oh, it's been a very popular story these past twenty years. Very dramatic—plays well on the stage!

"I wrote a poem about it myself, when the tale first arrived in Joppa." He sounded wistful. "Rather moving, as I remember."

"Ammon, you're a wise man. . . ."

"Tut, my boy." The poet looked embarrassed.

"Educated, familiar with history. Can you explain what happened to me tonight? For I swear by all the gods that less than an evening ago I was asleep on a beach on Seriphos and have no idea how I come to be here."

Ammon looked thoughtful as he sipped at his wine which, like himself, was well aged. "We are fairly certain it was not by boat. Nor, I would wager, by any other means mortal man might use." He turned serious.

"The gods of Olympus are unfathomable, their motives erratic, their methods mysterious. It is best to avoid their attention whenever possible, for those who come to their attention are as often as not punished rather than rewarded.

"My advice to you, Perseus, would be to treat this little shift of sleeping place as temporary, to return to the calm of Seriphos as quickly as you can, and to forget the entire matter. Treat it as a dream, my boy, and you will wake from this experience the healthier. That is what I would recommend."

"But what if I was brought here for a reason?"

"Reason or whim, what does it matter, so long as the gods trouble you no more?"

"My mother's last wish was that I should restore her honor and claim my birthright as heir to the throne of Argos. Perhaps Joppa would be a better place to begin than a remote little island. I am tired of moving slowly through life. Seriphos is a kind home, but a futureless one." He pushed his chair away from the table, stood, and began wandering around the chamber studying the dusty costumes and props.

"Better inertia than death," Ammon muttered, but Perseus did not hear him. "Well, my boy, if you are determined on this course . . . "

"I am."

". . . then you will need weapons, advice, counsel and knowledge. And something more important still."

"And what might that be?"

Ammon's tone shifted from serious to sprightly. "Something to wear." He gestured at Perseus's fisherman's loincloth. "Something rather more appropriate to a prince, even if he remains as yet only prince of a hopeful vision."

Leaving the table, he walked to a high pile of costumes. After several minutes of searching he excavated an embroidered royal cloak of the Tyrian purple for which Phoenicia was famed throughout the world.

Setting it across Perseus's shoulders, he moved the youth back until he was standing awkwardly before one of the prop thrones. The boy's expression spoke of youth and inexperience, but Ammon could see real courage there, and a burning desire to learn.

He nodded, satisfied at the sight thus presented. "That will do. Welcome to Joppa... *Prince* Perseus!" And he executed a mock bow.

Both men laughed, old poet and young prince, and each saw a little of himself in his companion.

Perseus removed the old loincloth and threw it away, to stand grinning in front of the throne. "Am I properly dressed, then?"

Ammon laughed so hard the tears ran down his face and salted his whiskers. "For success in the city, yes, but for a prince I fear still somewhat underclad. We have begun from the outside. Now we must dress inwards— unless you will settle for being prince only among the ladies."

They worked with the costumes by torchlight, joking and swapping tales as they sought to complete Perseus's attire. ...

There is always rage in a thunderstorm: black clouds shot through with lightning, unstable winds, capricious vortices of energy.

All that and more was reflected in the face of Zeus as he confronted Thetis, Hera, Aphrodite, and Athene. The anger in his voice ruffled the feathers of the owl seated on the shoulder of the goddess of wisdom, and the immortal bird sought shelter behind his mistress's long tresses.

"You set him down half-naked, alone, ignorant, and hungry outside a strange, accursed city!"

"You once said that chance would rule his future, Father Zeus." Thetis looked away from him, not quite able to meet the accusation in his eyes.

"This had nothing to do with chance, and well you know it!" He leaned back in the throne, fuming and fighting to control his temper. "This was a deliberate and malicious act unworthy of a goddess!"

"You accuse *me*?"

"And not wrongly, I think." He glared a moment longer at the sea goddess before turning his attention to the motionless statuette standing on the floor of the pulsing amphitheater. "Who else would have reason?" His gaze traveled over the other three. "And the rest of you have connived in this. I sense it."

"Nonsense," Hera said, staring back reprovingly. "We have done nothing."

"Precisely my point, Hera. In doing nothing you have allowed this unfortunate intrusion into the affairs of men. No reaction is the same as bestowing one's approval." He took in a deep breath and wind whistled outside on the mountain.

"Nevertheless, it is done. I cannot reverse it. Now truly will chance control events.

"But one thing is certain. He needs and now deserves, because of your actions, more than an actor's dyed cloak and a wooden sword to defend himself." He smiled warningly.

"I will shield him from otherwordly interferences, but he will be forced to defend himself against the threats of the Earth and his fellowman. I charge you all to provide him with suitable weapons. You claim to have done nothing. I now give you something to do.

"Athene, from you a proper helmet. Aphrodite, send him a sword suitable to his heritage—one that will not shatter at the first parry of an opponent. And should he misparry," he concluded, speaking now to Hera, "you will give him a shield. These he must have with all speed."

Bundling his robes about him he turned and stalked out of the chamber, to brood on the solitary throne which crowned the very crest of the mountain. There he would commune silently with his friends the winds and perhaps cast earthward the occasional angry thunderbolt for which he was famed among mortal man.

When he was long departed, Thetis unclenched her teeth and muttered in frustration, "All this anger and trouble for the love of Danae."

"No." Hera smiled knowingly. "Not for the love of Danae. Not for the love of any woman. So many have beguiled him that he couldn't possibly become so attached to one. No, it's simply his foolish pride in a handsome, half-mortal son. That is all he remembers, all that concerns him now, and that is what rouses him to such unusual solicitude." Her smile twisted.

"He would never admit that, of course. That would be a sign of weakness."

"Your husband can be curiously mortal at times," Aphrodite observed, tapping her lower lip with an exquisite finger. "All the faults of an ordinary human. But a great deal more stamina."

"What exactly do you mean?" Hera turned a sharp eye on her fellow immortal.

"Oh, don't play coy with us," Thetis said loftily. "Don't try to match your husband at the art of not admitting things you know. It is as you say . . . so many women." She shook her head in puzzlement.

"All these transformations and disguises he concocts to protect his identity and godly dignity while he seduces them. Imagine making love to a shower of gold!"

Aphrodite looked thoughtful, finally said in a languorous sigh, "It may have its merits, sister."

"To you anything has its merits!" Thetis

spoke sharply but not maliciously. "He becomes a bull, a swan— Why, once long ago he even tried to ravish *me*, disguised as a cuttlefish."

Aphrodite finished a catlike stretch and frowned. "I think I should prefer a shower of gold."

"Did he succeed?" Hera asked the question with more than casual interest.

"Certainly not." Thetis appeared insulted. "I have more will than to permit that, nor am I as vulnerable to such advances as a mere mortal."

"What did you do?" asked Athene, ever questioning.

"In the first place, cuttlefish are not among my favorite watery denizens. I could not, however, confront him as a goddess there in the depths. So I beat him at his own game. I turned myself into a shark. Cooled more than his ardor, I can tell you!"

The laughter that filled the chamber was rich and feminine, and in its own way even more human than Zeus's outrage.

It is in the nature of dust that it can seem a drab covering or a golden glaze, depending on its constituent components and the time of day. What had looked filthy during the night took on a warm luster with the rise of Apollo's chariot, a quality imparted to the old theater not by godly condescension but by the amount of mica in both its dust and building stones.

Birds appeared—the only audience the amphitheater now played host to—and began to play out their own small individual tragedies with the insects and the worms hiding in the weeds. A thousand little deaths occurred as the sun rose higher in the Mediterranean sky, and no playwright was present to document them.

Rock was already becoming hot to the touch when Perseus emerged from the entrance leading to the stairwell. He stretched, lifted his face to the morning sun. His belly was full; he'd found an erudite and interesting friend; he now knew where he was though not how he'd arrived there; and all in all the world seemed a far more hospitable place than it had the night before.

The nightmare had melted into a mere puzzle, and he'd always liked puzzles. The explanation for his present peculiar situation could surely not be better hidden than the secret places of Seriphos's tastier reef dwellers. Seeking it out might prove exciting.

How exciting, he could not begin to imagine.

In the fresh light of morning the amphitheater no longer appeared forboding. The scrub brush poking persistent frazzled crowns through the decaying masonry no longer looked like anxious fingers waiting to drag the unwary down to Hades. Flies and bees buzzed over the paving stones, the one hunting carrion, the other flowers.

Perseus inspected his false finery. The

short kilted tunic, the wide gilded belt and thonged sandals contributed to the illusion if not the reality of a true prince. The costume would surely make more of an impression on any people he met than would his dubious pedigree.

"Impression and appearance are everything in this world, my boy," Ammon had said the night before while they'd been scrounging up a royal wardrobe from among the costume finery. "Substance is nice but affects only the perceptive. For the great majority, impression is what matters."

This morning the young man did not convey an impression of royalty as he ran joyously down the steps into the arena and turned a couple of backflips for the sheer pleasure of it. He was exulting in a new day and the knowledge that, while displaced and alone, he was not mad.

Something among the broken columns and decapitated statues was shining into his eyes, making him blink. It was brighter than the sun. Raising a hand to ward off the glare, he tried to make out the source, but it was far too bright.

Hesitant, he glanced around the amphitheater in search of his newfound mentor. Ammon was not to be seen, still somewhere below in his subterranean haven. Something told Perseus that the glare did not arise from some forgotten piece of scenery or costume buckle.

Still trying to shield his eyes from the glare, he walked toward it. As the angle of his approach changed, the glare lessened and he was finally able to see its source—sources, rather, for there were three.

Among the statues ringing the amphitheater were those representing the major gods and goddesses. Aegyptian, Phoenician, Minoan and others mixed with the more familiar deities of Hellas. Origin notwithstanding, few had escaped unblemished, having been desecrated with varying degrees of imagination and obscenity by callous unbelievers.

Ahead of Perseus stood the damaged images of the goddesses Hera, Aphrodite and Athene. Scattered among them were the three sources of light which had brought tears to his eyes.

Against the chipped and fractured form of the goddess Hera lay a highly polished shield. A sword hung balanced in the cracked arms of Aphrodite, and a helmet sat askew on the mutilated head of wise Athene. Perseus was an intelligent lad, but just then it did not occur to him to wonder at this democratic distribution of artifacts. He was too absorbed by the mystery and wonder of the objects themselves.

As was natural for any young man of his age, he inspected the sword first. The chipped, cracked statue remained nothing more than a damaged hunk of marble as he carefully took the weapon from its arms.

It threw aside the sunlight with all the haughtiness of the goddess of love's own mirrors. The amphitheater might be old, the statues older, and Ammon positively archaic, but this weapon was new. Perseus was no smith, but even to his untrained eyes the sword looked to be a masterpiece of the forger's art. The blade was straight, flawless, and gleaming —it might have been tempered in the heart of the sun itself.

He'd handled swords on Seriphos, mostly in play, though at his mother's insistence he'd received serious instruction in the arts of warfare from an old soldier who'd retired to the island. A gruff, unfriendly sort, the old warrior had been warmed like everyone else by Perseus's good nature and open friendliness.

"The village folk say that you're an expert at war. How do you come to be considered an expert?" Perseus had asked one day when he'd been learning the use of spear and shield.

The old man had wiped sweat from his chin and grinned ruefully. "Boy, some day you'll learn that all old soldiers are experts in the art of war. If you're not an expert you never get to be old. . . ."

IV

Perseus considered that advice now as he studied the strange sword. There would be time enough later to consider how it came to be deposited here in the deserted theater.

He touched the edge with his left index finger and drew it back in surprise. But a more cautious second touch revealed that the blade was not heated, as he'd first thought, but was sharp beyond belief.

Searching the ground, he came up with a thick piece of wood that had once supported some painted backdrop for a Sophoclean tragedy. He took a casual slash at the section of post, curious to see how deeply the blade would penetrate.

To his considerable amazement the sword cut clean through the tough hardwood as though it were made of cheese. He was so startled that he dropped both pieces of wood and nearly cut off his own foot with the follow-through of the gentle swing.

"You're up with the sun, then. A wonderful morning, my young friend."

"More than wonderful," Perseus told the approaching playwright. His eyes were still held by the gleaming sword. "Magical would be a better word. Come close and see what wonder I have found."

Ammon threw aside the bone he'd been gnawing and came alongside. "Well?"

Perseus held out the sword, careful to keep the edge away from the old man. "I found this," he said, gesturing back over his shoulder, "here by the statue. There was no one around. The reflection caught my attention." He indicated the statue. "It was in her arms."

"A likeness of the goddess of love." Ammon sighed, looking at the statue. "Ill-treated by the rabble who sometimes infest the theater despite my tireless efforts to protect it.

"A much admired work once upon a time, but no longer maintained. I'm no stone mason. I've neither the skill nor the muscle to repair the damage. But you found this sword by it, you say?"

Perseus nodded. "In the statue's arms. It's not an ordinary sword, old friend. See?" He reversed it so that Ammon could take it by the handle. "Be careful. It cuts with all the gentleness of a kiss."

"The two are not always mutually exclusive," Ammon replied, eyes twinkling. He tilted his head slightly back and squinted as he examined the blade.

"Strange. I'd say it's neither bronze nor iron. It might almost be silver, but that would mean it's no working sword, and you say it has a fine edge?"

Perseus nodded vigorously.

"Then it's no kin to any metal I know." Ammon scratched his thinning hair.

Curious to see if the point was as sharp as Perseus insisted, he prodded a fallen marble column. Not only did the point not break off against the stone, it chipped away a chunk of marble as easily as if the column were a loaf of bread.

"By the gods!" Ammon looked respectfully at the blade.

"And there's more." Excitedly, Perseus pointed to the flanking statues. "Look, there's a shield, and over there a helmet on poor Athene."

Ammon moved from one statue to the next, carefully studying each artifact in turn. When he'd finished, his attention went back to the sword he still held.

"Perhaps I was right to mention the gods."

"These are only old statues."

"Yes, but this weaponry is not. No citizen of Joppa would abandon such valuable items. My cats would have warned me if someone had been poking around the theater last night. And we overheard no sounds of fighting. Besides, any victor would surely have taken such spoils as these away with him. We heard nothing.

"But the gods can be as silent as they can be noisy." He held the sword high and let the sun dance on the blade.

"Who else could have fashioned a sword that slices through solid marble without leaving so much as a blemish on the edge?"

"It is truly unnaturally sharp," Perseus agreed.

"Unnatural is the right word, I should think." He handed the weapon back to its discoverer. "Here. I want as little to do with the manifestations of the gods as possible."

"If the sword can do so much, then what about the helmet and the shield?"

"I prefer not to speculate," said Ammon dryly, "but surely they were placed here for a reason." He indicated the sword. "If that were an unnaturally facile stylus, then I'd worry about it. But the sword can only be intended for you, my boy. I suppose we'd better ... *you'd* better find out about the rest."

Perseus nodded enthusiastically. "I'll try the helmet, I think." He turned and started toward the cracked statue of Athene.

"No, try me first."

He turned, looked curiously at Ammon. "What did you say?"

"I didn't say anything." The poet's face was pale. "I wish I had. But it came from over there, by the statue of Hera. From the shield, I think, not from the statue."

Perseus remained motionless. "What do you think I should do, wise friend?"

"I think that when shields begin to talk, mere mortals would do well to pay attention to whatever they might say, my boy."

Perseus changed direction and approached the shield. Ammon followed reluctantly, wishing silently for the legs and wind of a twenty-year-old.

His young companion lifted the gleaming, round shield. The convex front was decorated with the raised likeness of a peacock. Unusual decoration for a war shield, Ammon thought.

"Turn me around," said the shield.

Perseus looked back at Ammon, who had no advice to give. Carefully the youth turned the shield, to reveal not the usual lining of leather and sheepskin padding but bare metal, polished to a mirrorlike finish. Both men leaned forward to stare at their own reflections.

"Curious," observed Ammon. "A shield without padding or lining. Only the armstraps."

"Nothing," agreed Perseus.

"Nothing at all."

"What about me?" came the voice once again.

Something was forming in the reflective inner surface. Ammon fought down a sudden urge to test his legs. As ever, his curiosity had the better of him. Perseus simply stood and stared, fascinated by the face crystallizing in the shield.

It was the wavering image of an old man, but one of much stronger constitution than Ammon. It was weatherworn and aged like a mountain, with a beard like gathering storm clouds. It floated in the shield as it talked to them.

"Perseus . . . Perseus . . . mark me, Perseus. Mark me well and never forget the words I have for you. These weapons are the gifts of the gods. Guard well this shield, for one day it will guard your life."

"Guard my life? When?"

"You will know when the day comes."

Ammon nodded mentally. Truly the gift of the gods, he thought sardonically, for only gods and writers love to terrorize and confuse straightforward speech with mystery and rhetoric.

"And the helmet," Perseus asked the face, "what of that? What does it do?"

"It has the power to render its wearer invisible," the face told him. *"There are all kinds of shields, Perseus, and the helmet is but another."*

"Invisible?"

"Invisible. Not there. Nonexistent to those who might harm you. That is the shield most men desire but few ever master. Guard it well." The face shimmered like a reflection in rippling water, and was gone.

"Wait, wait! Who are you?"

"Find and fulfill your destiny." This last admonition was barely audible.

Perseus put the shield, now a thing of only metal, back down on the stones. "What did it mean by that?"

"Who can say?" Ammon wore a rueful smile. "Many things, perhaps. In any case, a divine gift should never be questioned. Simply accepted."

"But I was taught that everything should be questioned."

"Then question the purpose, if you must question, but not the gift. Now ... let us see to this helmet."

Perseus moved to the statue of Athene, trailed by the anxious playwright. Carefully the youth removed the helmet from the head and slipped it onto his own. For an instant he was unchanged. Then the tall, muscular figure vanished like a forgotten dream. Only his voice remained to remind Ammon that he was not dreaming himself.

"Can you see me, Ammon?"

The playwright looked toward the source of the question, saw only stone seats and blue sky, blighted grass and a mockingly silent statue.

"No, nothing," he replied excitedly, "nothing of you at all." There was no immediate response and he turned in a nervous circle.

"Where are you? Don't play tricks on an old man, Perseus." Then he noticed the shifting patterns forming on the dusty floor of the theater.

"Ah, all I can see are your footprints. The

gods are truly remarkable! Even if maddeningly uninformative. They have given you the means to make yourself hidden from your fellowman, but have not told you why this might be necessary."

The footsteps began to move away, hurrying toward the amphitheater exit. The distance between them lengthened with every stride.

Panting hard and holding his tunic away from his feet, Ammon raced after the footprints.

"Perseus! Where are you going? Slow down and wait for me, boy."

"No time, friend Ammon. I'm going to Joppa, into the city."

"But it's too dangerous ... too soon for you! You don't know the ways of the city folk or how to get about. Impossible!"

The receding voice seemed to pause a moment, and said laughingly, "I'm invisible! You can see that. A moment ago you'd have sworn before all the gods that this was impossible too. But look at me now."

"You infernal imp, I can't *see* you now!" Ammon was furious both with the stubborn youngster and with his own failing strength. He stumbled to a halt, wheezing and wide-eyed.

A last exultant shout reached him from beyond the exit arch: "Then nothing's impossible!"

Maybe not, you young fool. Ah well, that

was important too, he mused. Invisibility's nice, but it's not as important as youth's eternal optimism. That was what made the boy so strong-headed: youth, not the gifts of the gods.

Perhaps it was for the best. Perseus would have to enter Joppa soon enough. He might as well do it while he was feeling so confident and pleased with himself. He would learn about the dangers and sorrows of the city soon enough.

Ammon thought back to his own first contacts with Joppa and other great cities, and how confident he had been in his own ability to conquer the world of stage and poetry. Time puts us each in our proper place, he thought. It will wear down Perseus eventually, as it does all men. Leave him to his youthful enthusiasm and happiness.

He turned to go back down to his study, but stopped as something bright caught his eye. He walked hastily to it, then turned and yelled toward the exit.

"Perseus, your sword!" But there was no answer, the fleet-footed youth having long since passed out of earshot.

The playwright turned once more, muttering tiredly. "Foolish, impetuous . . . why do the young never listen? When will they ever learn?"

He continued on to his study, bemoaning the vagaries of youth in the time-honored manner of the aged, which is to say fondly and without real bitterness.

There were greater cities in the ancient world than Joppa, cities of greater size and more enduring monuments. But there were at that time not many as prosperous.

Joppa rode high on the ministrations of its merchants, bold seafarers who sailed the length and breadth of the Mediterranean in search of new lands, new tales—and new markets. These fearless explorers touched distant Italy and far Hispania, made forays to the villages lining the sun-kissed coast of southern France-to-be, and dealt for ivory and slaves with the peoples of North Africa.

They carried the famous Tyrian purple dye throughout the ancient world, a color much sought after by kings and despots. They traded as far as ancient Britain and swapped beads and trinkets with the barbarians of that impossibly distant, primitive land. The amber they brought back from the Baltic decorated the necks of Joppa's most beautiful women. Even great Aegypt envied the city her fine walls and palaces.

Joppa was also a meeting place for distant caravans from the far deserts. Occasionally one could listen to a tired cameleer as he sat by the piers or in the marketplace and told tall tales of a land where the people had yellowish skins and slanted eyes, or of the ruins of a great city called Mohenjo-Daro.

The little alcove was momentarily unwatched, so none saw the royal figure that magically appeared therein. Perseus removed the helmet and tucked it beneath one arm. His eyes roamed over the thick walls, the Assyrian-influenced statuary, and the polyglot mob that milled in the streets.

Eventually his gaze turned to the vast open area off to his left. He started toward the central marketplace. No one stared or thought to question him. In Joppa, Greeks were as common as olives.

He blended naturally into the crowd, differing from those around him only because he was handsomer than the average and smelled far better than most. Camels, merchants and peddlers jostled for room all around him, arguing, fighting, bargaining, and cursing in a multitude of tongues.

The marketplace backed like a lake up to a high, curving archway. Palms and an occasional massive cedar offered shade, together with the transient awnings of the vendors. Beyond the arch lay the main square of the city. A thin pillar of black smoke rose from its center.

This open area was devoid of merchants and gave every indication of being used for ceremonial functions. Presently it was filled with an anxious throng of men, women and children. Their conversation was low and nervous, their attitudes suggestive of a not entirely healthy anticipation.

The buildings and walls enclosing the square showed the African and Asiatic in-

fluences that had spilled over into the Middle
East. Some of the decorations did not reflect
the gentlest of those influences.

More than a dozen soldiers ringed the
large bonfire that blazed in the center of the
square. They kept the crowd at a distance.
Curiously, their expressions hinted that they
were as unhappy as the people.

Perseus moved through the arch and
paused. An officer of the royal guard leaned
casually against a nearby wall. Perseus started
through the crowd toward him, reasoning that
he would be the likely one to have an explanation for whatever ceremony was taking place.
It did not occur to Perseus that the soldier
might regard his questioner with any suspicion.

The babble of the expectant masses became a worried buzz. Straining to see over the
shifting heads as he continued working his way
toward the soldier, Perseus noted a cluster of
priests standing near the fire. Standing alone
and apart from them was the striking figure of
a mature woman. She appeared to be in her
early forties, a regal silhouette clad in rich attire, laden with jewels and gold.

"Who is that?" he asked one of the onlookers.

The man did not turn his gaze from the
spectacle. "Stranger indeed is he who does not
know the glorious Cassiopeia, queen of Joppa
and ruler of all Phoenicia! Where be you from,
boy?" he asked curiously.

Perseus quickly moved away without answering, but kept his eyes on the woman. She was standing as motionless and straight as a column of marble. Trying to see the details of her face, he thought he could sense more than just beauty there. There was ambition, and desire, and a great capacity to rule. His mother had shown him how to recognize such things. A queen indeed, he thought.

At last he was able to make out the object of the queen's attention, of the priests' and of the crowd's.

In the center of the bonfire, concealed from view until now by the post and thick smoke, was a burning man.

His stomach turned slightly and his expression fell. All the initial wonder and glory of Joppa, all the magnificence of the city and its teeming markets were wiped out by that single gruesome sight. Such sacrifices and cruelties were not unusual in Perseus's world, but they were certainly new to him personally.

He watched several moments more, until the thing tied in the middle of the blaze was no longer human. Then he resumed his walk until at last he stood beside the still lounging soldier.

The guard had reached that point in his military career where he no longer entertained false illusions about promotion or glory. His uniform and armor were clean but not spotless. Sandals and sword both looked worn and well used. He was a blocky, dark-haired veteran of many battles, as indicated by his surfeit of scars.

To Perseus he looked Macedonian. He might even be from farther south than that mountainous province. A fellow kinsman, even. Despite any such ethnic relationship, Perseus knew this man to be a loyal soldier of his city.

While Perseus was studying his quarry, the soldier was also sizing up the young man standing next to him. Despite his curiosity about the richly clad young stranger, the soldier held his silence and his pose. In one hand he held a horsehair whisk. This was in constant, irregular motion, doing futile but hopeful battle with the flies that infested the marketplace. At the moment, it was the smoke from the fire that was keeping those pests down.

Unable to restrain himself any longer, he turned to stare into Perseus's face. After a moment's hesitation, he asked, "A stranger here? I can't identify the markings of your raiment, young sir, but your skin and face mark you as Greek."

"I am that," Perseus replied readily. "As for my clothing, it is of no particular significance except to my mind."

"A good country to give allegiance to." Despite his appearance it was clear to Perseus that this officer was better educated than most of his kind.

"I am a stranger to Joppa, yes." Perseus

nodded toward the bonfire, his expression twisting. "And a stranger to sights like that. Why is the man put to so horrible a death? Was he a criminal?"

· The soldier shook his head. "No. It is all a part of a nasty business, my young friend." The officer ﹒pointed toward the blackened corpse, now hanging limp from the center pole. "He was a suitor for the hand of the Princess Andromeda." His hand moved to point out another figure. "That tall woman over there now conferring with the priests is her mother, Queen Cassiopeia of Joppa."

Perseus looked confused and sounded a little angry. "I don't understand. If he committed no crime save that of seeking a princess's hand in marriage, why should he be condemned to death? Is it a crime in Joppa to seek love?"

"Love!" The officer laughed. "You are young indeed, my friend."

Upset, Perseus started to turn away. The soldier reached out to stay him.

"Nay, I meant no offense, friend." He smiled. "My name is Thallo, of the city guard. Do not think I or anyone else in Joppa takes joy in these spectacles, least of all the queen."

"Then why do they occur?"

"I do not entirely understand myself. These are strange times, my friend. Andromeda was destined from birth to marry a great lord named Calibos. This was arranged, you understand. I did not know the fellow myself, but from what marketplace and barracks gossip indicates he was handsome of face and body, but dark in mind and heart. An evil, powerful man.

"As the rumors go, he offended one of the gods—no difficult task, given their temperaments."

"Beware of blasphemy, Thallo, or you may offend them as did this Calibos."

The old soldier shrugged uncaringly. "I'm not afraid of the gods. One quickly loses respect for them on the battlefield. Their favorites seem to be chosen indiscriminately. I've seen them let too many good men die and too many tyrants come to power.

"But it seems no one regretted the punishment of this man Calibos."

Perseus considered. "It seems strange to me that a queen would promise her daughter an evil marriage."

Thallo tried to explain. "Did you not understand what I meant when I said the marriage was 'arranged'? No, I see you are not familiar with such things.

"The marriage promises were exchanged when both the princess and the lord were infants. Calibos's true nature did not reveal itself until he grew much older. By then it was much too late for the queen to break her promises."

"How did the gods punish him, if he indeed offended one of them?"

"Turned him into a reflection of Hades, I'm told. Part man, part beast, and part something no decent soldier like myself would ever hope to see. I've fought forty campaigns, my young friend, and I'm afraid of no man. But this Calibos is no longer a man. Those few who claim to have espied him out in his lair have a hard time talking of it." Thallo slapped angrily at one biting insect undeterred by either the fading smoke or the steady swish of the whisk.

"Well," he continued, "it takes no oracle to imagine what happened afterward. One sight of Calibos as he truly was, his outer self now reflecting the inner, and the good Andromeda understandably refused steadfastly to marry him. Queen Cassiopeia, bless her, was torn between a promise decades old and love for her own daughter. Eventually, despite what the bets in the barracks said would happen, she sided with her daughter and called the marriage off.

"Well, the priests were called in fast to read the signs and omens and generally do their usual mischief. They declared that the goddess Thetis, the patron goddess of Joppa, by the way, was angry. There's some loose talk that this Calibos is somehow related to the goddess. So that made things doubly difficult.

"Since then, it seems that any man can present himself as a suitor for the princess. But the courting is cursed by Calibos; therefore, by declaration of the priests, any man who fails the marriage testing is fuel for warming."

"Have many failed?"

Thallo nodded somberly. "Too many."

"I wonder that any would continue to try."

Thallo's face brightened and he looked wistful. "Andromeda's very beautiful, my friend. Beautiful as a goddess. I've seen her myself, and she's worth the risk.

"Besides, whoever succeeds in passing the test and marrying her will eventually become king—the queen has no other children—and rule the city and the whole kingdom."

"If there's so much to be gained," asked Perseus innocently, "and you say she's worth dying for, why not try for her yourself?"

"Who . . . me?" Thallo held his sides and almost dropped his whisk as he roared with laughter.

"Bless me, my young friend, but I'm near as ugly as this Calibos himself! She'd never have me. And I'm not so old that I'm ready to give up my life. I don't like the odds. Seen too many good men fail.

"No, I'll wait out my pension, thanks, and retire to my family's fruit orchard near Tyre. Besides, I'm already wedded. I don't need a great beauty and a kingdom to keep me happy. Some men might."

Perseus was still listening, but now he was staring down into the crowd surrounding the queen. "Where is she, then?"

"Not here." Thallo moved away from his wall to gesture past the square and the enclosing ramparts. "Over there, in the highest tower of the palace, above the smoke and stench.

She's got no stomach for this carrying-out of the curse's provisions.

"It's said she will no longer eat or speak, in protest of this damnable ritual. So she remains up there alone—away from these accursed, hell-sent, blood-gutted, putrid, bloated swarms of rotten marsh flies!" and he danced violently as something attacked the back of his neck.

Perseus stepped back. No one was watching, and Thallo was momentarily occupied. All other eyes were still on the center of the square, where a tall priest was reciting a last litany over the ashes of the most recent royal suitor.

Slipping the helmet over his head, Perseus turned to depart. Thallo turned to continue the conversation, startled to discover that his friend had vanished.

Nice enough young fellow, that stranger, he mused. Now, where has he disappeared to? A naive young man like that could run into trouble in a city as frenetic and sophisticated as Joppa.

On the other hand, old soldier, he told himself, was it not he who asked the questions and you who willingly supplied all the answers? Maybe he isn't quite as innocent as he seems.

No matter. He turned back to the square, the conversation forgotten. What mattered now was not catching the eye of the queen; that, and preserving at least a little blood from these damnable marsh flies.

Marketplaces are wonderful, Perseus had decided by that night. You can find anything you need in them: food, clothing, drink . . . and information. Even information detailing the layout of a palace. Queen Cassiopeia was well liked by her people. Many of them had sought and been granted audience with her inside the confines of the great palace. A few of these fortunate supplicants had good memories of the physical layout.

That information was passed on to him with surprising readiness. His innocent face and mannerisms, his curiosity and apparent harmlessness had always stimulated in others a desire to help him, and to show off their own knowledge and wisdom. So he'd had no trouble sketching out a crude plan of the palace's interior and then making use of it.

Once he almost stumbled into the royal kitchens, a region of wondrous aromas which he'd been loath to depart empty-handed. But he had no time to stop and snack.

Now he found himself crouching behind an enormous marble urn in a long corridor. Ahead to his right should be a guardroom, and beyond it, storage and cleaning rooms. On the far left at the end of the hall would be a stairway leading up to a square tower.

He walked softly down the corridor, ever watchful not for the sharks of Seriphos's reef now, but for antagonists of fewer but longer teeth. There was noise from the guardroom, laughter and easy conversation. No one challenged him.

A single guard had been standing watch by the stairway while Perseus had hidden behind the urn, but now moved toward the guardroom, called by his companions. The soldier hesitated, certain he had heard footsteps. But a careful inspection of the corridor showed no one. He shrugged, turned, and entered the guardroom.

Behind him the invisible Perseus resumed his walk toward the stairs.

The doors there were unlocked, the alcove beyond deserted. A second set of doors at the top of the stairs was likewise unbarred. He pushed inward and found himself staring into a chamber larger than he'd expected to find.

It was sparsely furnished, decorated only by an occasional vase or sculpture. There was a sumptuous dressing table, several mirrors, and an open chest containing clothing. Across the chamber was a raised marble platform and on it, a huge bed.

The room was cool since the tower's height enabled it to catch the sea breezes which passed over the steaming city below. They blew in through a large open arch. A balcony extended outward from the opening.

The bed was enveloped by filmy curtains of near transparent silk brought all the way from distant Cathay on the backs of camels and mules. Men and animals had perished so that a princess might be spared the inconvenience of mosquito and fly bites while she slept.

The door swung farther inward, then closed as if by magic. There were quiet footsteps and the clink of metal on metal. Perseus decided the chamber was safe. There was no other hint of movement within.

He took off the helmet. If it were possible he wanted the princess to see him as clearly as he hoped to see her. Moving lithely toward the bed while still keeping a wary eye ready for unexpected chambermaids, he mounted the marble platform and parted the pastel gauze.

Andromeda lay clad in a gown of material only slightly darker, though no less soft, than the screening silks. She was smaller than Perseus had envisioned her after seeing her mother the queen, though clearly no child.

Her hair was draped loosely across her pillow, forming a golden aura more brilliant than any crown. An air of disturbed innocence seemed to emanate from her sleeping form. Aloof from the murderous ceremonies in the square she might be, but her expression hinted that she was not unaffected by them. Unable to alter those ceremonies, she had withdrawn from the world that countenanced them.

I will bring you back, he abruptly promised himself. You are too beautiful to hide here in a tower of cold stone. I will see you out in the world again, free to shine like Apollo's chariot, free of the fear I see in your sleeping face. Let me do this for you and I will myself then be forever happy.

He reached in and down toward her cheek, bent on assuring himself that she truly existed and was not merely some godly vision.

His hand never touched her.

A noise suddenly came to him from the exposed balcony, a vast rushing sound, the echo of disturbed air, the beating of immense wings.

Then something coughed and made a sound like two ships grinding hulls. Carefully he turned from the bed and the princess and looked uncertainly toward the arch. There was something enormous out there and it was moving closer.

Never taking his eyes from that now shadowed arch, he moved back to where, though hidden by a column, he could still see outside.

There was a nearly full moon that night: it showed him too much of the thing that had lighted on the balcony's carved balustrade. . . .

V

In its beak it held a small golden cage. That vast maw could have swallowed the cage in a single gulp. The sharp beak glowed yellow brown in the moonlight, stained with the blood of untold numbers of corpses. Back of the beak were comparatively tiny eyes the color of previous meals, dark red and glowing with an unholy inner light.

It made a noise, a deep-throated parody of a caw. Like a grotesque backdrop lifted intact from some dark play, it shifted its awkward, massively taloned feet. Marble crumbled slightly beneath its vast bulk, but the balustrade held firm.

Though big enough to lift an elephant, the enormous vulture displayed a gentle touch as it set the cage down on the balcony. Glaring into the chamber whose entrance was too narrow for its body, it cawed again.

Perseus hugged the column and stared in fascination at the great bird. It crooned a third time, a definite rhythm to the call.

Another sound caught his attention, and he turned to the veiled bed. The princess had turned on her side. As he watched, she moaned softly, her eyes closed.

The vulture continued to call, insistent and demanding. Its head bobbed as it tried to peer deeper into the bedchamber. Perseus hurriedly slipped the helmet of invisibility over his head lest the bird espy him behind the column.

Then it happened.

A second Andromeda had materialized on the bed, rising like a ghost from the moaning body of the sleeping princess. At first no denser than the thin curtains veiling the bed, the outline gradually accumulated substance as it left the princess entirely and began walking slowly toward the archway. Even at its densest, though, it remained undeniably a shadow of the real form.

The vulture shifted uneasily on the balustrade as the surrogate Andromeda came into view. The figure's eyes were as tightly shut as those of the girl on the bed, its expression one of resignation as it walked slowly toward the cage. The golden door, expecting her, opened by itself.

Her movements as mechanical as those of a clock, the second Andromeda entered the cage and seated herself on the golden chair within. Her hands gripped the arms of the chair and a faint look of nervousness crossed her somnolent face.

A rushing wind filled the chamber and fluttered the curtains encircling the bed as the vulture rose from the wall. It hovered carefully above the cage, its talons delicately grasping the perch attached to the top. Then it beat harder at the air, fighting to raise not the flimsy cage but its own mass.

It vanished northeastward, behind a cloud.

Perseus stepped out from behind the concealing column, the helmet once more cradled beneath his arm. He moved cautiously to the archway, in time to catch sight of the great bird's outline for a moment before it disappeared over the horizon.

But the cause of the dream he'd just witnessed remained behind, solid and real as his own being. He found himself standing again by the side of the bed.

There the princess still slept her unnatural sleep. A second time he reached out, and this time nothing interrupted him from gently touching the motionless face. The princess did not respond, did not move.

"Andromeda," he whispered hopefully. There was no reaction, and he really hadn't expected any. He smiled down at the delicate, troubled face.

"Once I was told that I should have to

search and search, as do all men, to find my destiny. My search is at an end. I have found it now."

Impulsively, he bent as if to kiss her, but caught himself with his lips only inches from her own. Affected as she was by some evil spell, might not an unexpected kiss or touch awaken her at a possibly dangerous time?

His smile returned. Magician he was not, but he felt certain no kiss of love could harm another. He touched his mouth to hers, feeling a faint, warm exhalation that assured him she was still alive, no matter what portion of her had been carried off by the vulture. She did not react.

As he pulled away he wondered what had happened to her, what had thrown her into so divisive a sleep. What role did the great bird play in this? Was it doing the bidding of Calibos, or Thetis, or even perhaps someone else involved in the tangled affairs of Joppa?

Too complex for a mere fisherman to puzzle out, he decided. More experienced minds than my own are needed if sense is to be made of this puzzle, and if the princess is to be restored to health and happiness. I can give her the last, but only if she regains the other first.

More than knowledge would be required, too. The unraveling of the mystery would require someone with imagination as well as learning.

Fortunately, he knew just such an individ-

· ual. Persuading him to help might be another matter, however. . . .

Ammon looked up from the scroll he'd been studying. It was midday but the candles still burned to light the subterranean study.

"If you'd remembered to take your sword, perhaps you might have been able to do something positive, instead of standing there gawking like one of the palace statues!"

Perseus paced the cluttered room like a caged antelope. "That's not the kind of reaction I expected from an educated man like you, old friend."

"Education is always better applied in such matters with the point of a sword, my boy. Especially when one has the use of the sword you've been given."

"It wouldn't have made any difference, Ammon. Even if I'd had a weapon, there was no sense in attacking the monster. The real princess still slept in her bed. I saw her, left her there—asleep as before and as real as my own hand. Yet I saw her double go in the cage." He made an angry gesture, sweeping his hand toward the playwright.

"What if I had killed the bird? What might have happened to the second Andromeda and thence to the real one left behind in the bed? I might have done more damage than help. I thought it better to wait and ask advice than to act rashly."

Ammon nodded his approval. "Young you are, but you've a cooler head than this old one. Yes, you're quite right, Perseus. We need to know more before killing can be done.

"Most importantly we must find out who is controlling the bird and drawing forth the substance of the poor princess. There lies the danger. Wars are lost when kings fall, not a few of their soldiers. The vulture is obviously servant and not instigator."

"Who do you think is responsible? I thought Calibos, or possibly Thetis or another immortal who carries a vendetta against Joppa or its queen."

"Tell me more of this other Andromeda, the one carried off in a golden cage."

Perseus thought back to the previous night. "It was her very shape and form, down to the last detail of mouth, the final curl of her hair."

"You remember well," Ammon said, smiling slyly. "You must have studied her most carefully."

The sarcasm was lost on the reminiscing Perseus. "Even her sleeping gown was the same; yet, she was like a dark shadow, a sleepwalker—a ghost and yet more than that."

"We know she was not the latter, for ghosts are memories of the dead and you tell me you left the girl on the bed still warm and breathing."

"That's right."

"Then I would venture to guess the second

figure was what the astrologers and court magicians call an astral emanation. It is this image of her real self—her soul or spirit or astral shell or whatever you want to call it—that has been possessed and is being controlled by another." He looked thoughtful for a long moment. When he spoke again it was with conviction.

"Calibos *must* be the one behind this. No goddess or god would operate in so indecisive a manner, not when they could as easily command the real Andromeda. Everything you have described to me bespeaks the actions of a subtle, devious mind unwilling to let life continue naturally.

"Calibos was denied marriage to the real Andromeda. From what I have heard it would be characteristic of him to hold on to anything of the princess he can. Surely he is the one who is controlling this small portion of her." He looked sharply at Perseus.

"It is a small thing, but . . . which way did the vulture fly? Did you notice the direction?"

"It vanished into clouds, but from the time it left its perch on the castle wall it flew steadily northeastward."

"Ah!" Ammon's fist bounced off the rickety old table. "Then that settles it. That way lie the swamps and the lair of the Lord of the Marsh. Our friend Calibos."

"It seems clear enough, then," said Perseus determinedly. "We must find or make a way to follow the vulture so that I can be sure of freeing the princess without harm."

"If and when it appears to the princess again?"

"Yes ... but how are we going to follow a creature that flies through the air? Perhaps on horseback? A good rider might track so enormous a bird from below."

Ammon shook his head. "Not once it entered the swamps. Even if the night were perfectly clear you'd still soon fall behind." A glint of excitement crept into Ammon's expression.

"But what you say puts me in mind of another possibility. One that just might offer us a chance, although remote, I grant you. But, by the gods, it would be a chance worth taking!" He eyed Perseus speculatively.

"You have the spirit, the youth and the strength, and from what I know of you already, I am certain you have the courage. Whether you also have the skill remains to be seen. What I have in mind will require the skill and tenacity of a god."

"I'm no god, Ammon—just a man. But if you think we should try this thing and that it will help me help the princess, I'll surely do my best."

Ammon was smiling. "Which just may be good enough, my young friend. Love is a powerful stimulant."

"When and where?"

"Tonight," the old playwright responded instantly. "To the northeast of the city. By the Wells of the Moon, the gods willing—or indifferent, which is preferable because it's safer."

The moon was a globular yellow white lamp suspended in the sky. It was bright enough to show Ammon and Perseus the way through the quiet, shallow pools and the occasional thick copse of brush. The low region they were traversing was not swampy but boasted dense growth without the unhealthy atmosphere farther north.

Ancient trees shaded the pools and thick creepers and vines gave them a solemn appearance in the moonlight, the epiphytes trailing like a maiden's hair in the still water. Most of the insects were asleep, though the isolated buzz of a mosquito or drone of a frog would sometimes echo through the night air. There was no wind. The scenery looked as if it had lain untouched for a thousand years.

One particularly large pool was the focus of the efforts of the two men. They crawled patiently to its edge, using the gnarled, twisted roots of the great trees to conceal themselves, though there seemed nothing around to warrant such caution. The insects were busy with mundane matters; the frogs did not care.

In the moonlight the surface of the pool turned to quicksilver, fragmenting whenever a rare breeze stirred the placid surface. Stars shone bright as gold dust against the velvet sky, flanking the beaming moon.

Perseus regarded the glowing orb a moment and saw fit to offer a brief invocation to the moon goddess Artemis, that she might continue to provide them with a clear night through the bright reflection of her own beauty. He'd thought often of Artemis. She'd always seemed such a solitary goddess, transcribing her own distinct path through the universe. He wondered if, as the stories said, her skin was truly the color of fresh milk.

Ammon gestured toward the pool, drawing him out of his reverie. "When the full moon shines on this water, then they say that Pegasus, the last of the winged horses, will sometimes come to drink."

Perseus was carefully checking over the thick rope they'd brought with them, making sure one more time that no knots or kinks had developed in the line.

Hours passed and he had checked the rope until he was sick of the sight of it. Once a buck and his doe appeared like beige wraiths to sip delicately at the fresh water, and Perseus watched with silent pleasure. When they left, the Wells of the Moon seemed empty of all life. Would the great winged stallion never appear?

"Listen," he whispered at last.

Ammon had fallen asleep against the crook of a root and Perseus quickly shook him awake.

"Listen . . . no, look there!"

There was a rushing sound, but it might well have been the wind in the branches.

"I see nothing, boy." Damn these old eyes, Ammon cursed to himself.

"There!" Perseus crouched as low as possible against the shielding tree. "From beyond the dark edge of the moon. Pegasus!"

The stallion shone as white as the chalk Perseus used to pinch from the cliffs of Seriphos. Like a fluttering white leaf, the magnificent animal spiraled lazily out of the stars. Halting in midair, it began to circle the Wells of the Moon.

Perhaps it was playing a game of tag with its own reflection in the waters below. More likely it was making a careful inspection of the terrain before descending. No doubt it was still mindful of the depredations Calibos had once wreaked on its cousins, and was still wary of touching the treacherous earth.

Eventually, satisfied with its inspection or game or both, it folded its pale wings and settled gracefully by the sloping shore on the far side of the pool. It looked once to left and right before trotting down to the water's edge.

Carefully Perseus unstrapped his helmet while cautioning Ammon to keep his head down.

At the distant whisper, the winged horse lifted its head, glancing around nervously. Both men froze. After a long moment of testing the air, the stallion dipped its head once again. This time it began to drink.

Perseus slipped the helmet over his head and promptly vanished. Ammon handed the coil of rope to empty air, felt it taken by an unseen hand. Only footprints revealed Perseus's path as he moved out from behind the tree.

Reeds and other tall water grasses swayed

gently, in the light breeze. It blew toward Perseus, for which he was grateful. The stallion could not see him, but surely it could still smell, and might bolt at the scent of man.

It did not notice the reeds that parted as if at a gust of wind, and continued to drink. Settling to ground as infrequently as possible, it was quite thirsty when it did so and concentrated now on drinking its fill.

Perseus moved nearer, paused and readied the rope. Invisible or not, he knew he'd only have one throw before the stallion fled. His first toss would be his only one.

Again the horse lifted a curious head. Its ears pricked forward, straining to hear a repeat of the breaking reed it thought it had sensed nearby. But there was nothing in sight and no smell of another large creature in the night air. Yet the sound had been distinct. Confused, the horse turned away from the pool.

Perseus whirled the loop, hoping the slight whistling noise it made would not startle the stallion further. Just there, he thought excitedly. No need to wait any longer: the throw would be on the mark or it would miss. He let the loop fly.

It jumped like a snake from the concealment of the reeds and landed neatly around the horse's muscular neck. Startled by the sudden constriction, Pegasus reared, whinnying in shock and surprise.

Perseus pulled the loop tight, keeping his attention on the sharp hooves that tore up the earth in front of him as they sought an unseen enemy.

One pull yanked Perseus violently forward, but he couldn't spare a hand to grab for the helmet that tumbled from his head. Now the stallion could see its antagonist, and struck with angry forefeet at the now visible figure.

But Perseus had dodged hooves before. Without letting the rope slacken he managed to stay well out of range of the pawing feet.

Frustrated and frightened, the stallion wheeled away from its enemy and galloped in the opposite direction. The sudden maneuver caught Perseus off guard, and he had no time to admire the horse's cleverness. Somehow he managed to hang onto the rope as the stallion dragged him along the bank of the pool. He was grateful that the water's edge was thick with soft ferns and rushes, not the thorn bushes and cacti of his island home.

"Hang on, boy!" Ammon had bolted from the cover of the tree roots and was splashing and wading awkwardly around the rim of the pool after the combatants.

Pegasus began to gallop in circles, since the taller trees soon shut off any path of escape ahead and other pools did the same to each side. Breath steamed from his nostrils and his eyes were wild as he fought and bucked to shake off the restraining rope around his neck.

Ammon reached them, nearly fell, and barely managed to dodge to one side as the horse abruptly changed its direction and tried to run him down. By now Perseus, scratched and filthy but still full of fight, had managed to get back on his feet. He stumbled along in the horse's wake.

There was a stump coming up on his right. A quick prayer it was not rotten and . . . now!

The loop he'd made caught fast, quivered, and held tight around the stump. The stallion's head bent back and with a violent neigh it came to a halt.

Perseus had no time to exchange pleasantries and Ammon was too tired to, as the youth passed him the end of the rope.

"Try and make another loop around the stump if he gives you enough slack!" Perseus yelled to the breathless playwright. "Whatever you do, hold fast. You must hold!"

Ammon hardly had the strength to nod. Perseus took up the end of the rope, and using it for a guide, worked his way forward, dividing his attention between the horse's back and its dangerous hooves.

Pegasus turned suddenly, but this time he did not charge. Instead he stood quite still, ears laid back, lips curled to reveal his teeth; vapor steamed from his flaring nostrils: man and horse regarded each other expectantly.

Ammon struggled to wind another loop of the rope around the tree stump, occasionally throwing an anxious glance toward Perseus. That the youth could avoid those slashing hooves had been amply shown. But if the rope should snap unexpectedly . . .

Perseus shook himself free of his temporary daze by breaking his gaze away from the stallion's. There was death in those eyes, but also promise.

I have the catch in my net, he told himself, and it's more dangerous than I dreamed. But I would be a coward to let it go now.

He continued working his way carefully along the rope toward the motionless horse.

"Steady," he called softly, in as unaffected a voice as he could manage. "Steady, great one, steady and easy." He started whistling to it, as he'd learned to do with horses and mules as a child.

No truce was evident in those angry eyes, but the ears pricked up at the peculiar sound.

"That's a good fellow, isn't that a nice tune?" He whistled a few more bars. "Almost makes you want to go to sleep. . . . steady."

He was almost within reach of the graceful white head. His eyes once more bored into those of the horse, but his mind did not fog as it had a few moments earlier.

"Steady. . . ."

He ducked quickly. The sharp teeth just grazed his upper back. Ah, prince of horses, he thought with an exultant burst of energy, you are clever, and you are fast. But you are not so clever as I!

As the teeth had darted for him, he'd gone down and forward. By the time the head twisted to snap at his rising legs it was already too late. Perseus was seated on the broad back, one hand locked in the thick mane. With the other he drew the sword of Aphrodite. . . .

And to Ammon's considerable astonishment, cut the binding rope in half.

The old poet tumbled backward as the tension on the rope was abruptly released. He rolled in the dirt and grasses, trying to stay clear of the powerful legs now released to kick or run free.

He needn't have worried. Pegasus was far too concerned with the startling new sensation of a man on his back to worry about anything else. For several minutes he plunged and reared, bucked and kicked, trying to dislodge the alien weight and presence. Then other instincts took over.

Spreading powerful wings, the stallion struggled into the air. He lifted, touched ground again, and then began a steady climb as he adapted to the extra weight.

"Hold on, boy!" Ammon shouted as he got to his feet. His eyes were wide, his blood racing faster than it had in years. It was as though he and not the youth were trying to gain control of the flying horse, and he urged Perseus on with all the strength in his frail old body.

"Keep his head up, don't let him spin on you!"

It was doubtful whether Perseus heard Ammon's admonishments. He was too busy hanging on with legs and hands as the stallion soared high over the treetops. Flying turned out to be not so very different from diving, so he experienced no vertigo. But he knew that this was far more dangerous than swimming. If he were to relax his grip for even a moment, he would soon be little more than a stain upon the earth.

Pegasus dipped to his left, then his right. He dove toward trees and pulled up at the last second. Once he did a double loop and if Perseus had been hanging on with only his hands he probably would have fallen. But his powerful legs dug tight into the horse's flanks and the momentary pull did not dislodge him.

Ammon danced with frustration and worry as he watched these tortuous maneuvers. Perseus was young and strong, but no human muscles could endure forever the forces the stallion was subjecting them to. Fortunately, neither could equine muscles. Pegasus was tiring also.

There were no more loops or twists, no more violent dips and turns. Gradually the path through the sky became smoother, the acrobatics less extreme. Now and then the wingbeats would cease altogether and the horse would rest while gliding.

Experimentally, the exhausted Perseus used hand and leg to urge the horse leftward. Nothing happened. He tried again, speaking calmly to it while exerting pressure.

This time the horse tucked its left wing slightly in and down and they banked in the desired direction. Perseus eased off and their path straightened out. Now to the right this time . . . gently, gently.

Once the glowing white head turned and stared back at him. It wore an expression of uncertainty. The naked fury Perseus had first encountered had faded, replaced by something akin to acceptance. The stallion had not turned suddenly docile. Perseus doubted so spirited and independent a creature ever would. But it had become manageable.

He had won the aerial stallion's respect. Now he could proceed to the less arduous but no less important task of winning its friendship.

He experimented with other commands. Each time, the horse responded more rapidly and with greater confidence. It was willing to be taught.

Midair commands were simple enough. Perseus had grown up knowing the ways of horses and how to direct them. But he did not know a command which would make one land like a bird.

"Down!" he finally urged the stallion. At the same time he tried pushing down hard with both hands on the back of its neck. "Down." He pressed again. The horse dipped a little lower before leveling off. Perseus repeated the command and the movement, this time keeping the pressure on.

Pegasus glided smoothly toward the ground. Flushed with success, his rider used two commands simultaneously, trying to make the stallion bank left while descending. It responded immediately, almost enthusiastically, as though realizing for the first time that it had found a wonderful new game.

They were just above the surface, near the pond where Ammon stood waiting. "Hup!" Perseus took his hands off the ironlike neck, pulled gently on the mane. The horse backed air with its great wings, nearly knocking poor Ammon down again, and touched down as lightly as a hummingbird.

Carefully Perseus slid off the back, his hands still entwined in the mane. But Pegasus was as tired as he. It showed no signs of bolting, stood quietly nodding its head and breathing hard. There was no telltale tenseness in its neck muscles.

Slowly Perseus slipped his fingers free of the mane, patted the quivering neck. The horse bent and inhaled the fragrance of several night-blooming flowers. Then it began to eat.

"The most wonderful stallion in the world," Perseus murmured reverently as Ammon hobbled over. "Not another like it." His gaze went skyward.

"Ah, Ammon, my friend, to ride in the emptiness between earth and stars, to feel the wind in your face ... I wish I were a poet like you, so that I could properly describe the sensation."

"And I wish I were a young man like you, so that I could experience it," Ammon replied, breathing harder than the horse. "You felt no fear, then?"

"Me? Why, of course!" His smile softened

and he looked away. "At first I was utterly terrified. If I'd been given the chance I think I might have given up, let go. But the one place Pegasus did not fly me was close to the ground. I had to tame him or die." He gazed admiringly at the stallion as he talked.

"But once he sensed that I meant him no harm, when he felt comfortable with me, he relaxed, as did I. He is responsive to command and willing to obey, as smart a horse as ever I've ridden."

Pegasus looked up at him, his mouth full of flowers, and whinnied. He nudged Perseus with his muzzle. All the rage had gone from his noble face.

"See, he is more than responsive," said Ammon delightedly. "He likes you. Horse or men, it's all the same when it comes to friendship and understanding. He speaks to you with actions instead of words, but they are just as comprehensible."

Perseus nodded, wiping sweat from his face. He stumbled once and Ammon looked alarmed.

"You all right my boy? How do you feel?"

"Thirsty."

"I dare say. Excitement will dry a body out faster than the desert sun at midday. You sweated across half the sky, may the stars forgive you! I could do with something wet and cold myself. But we've neither amphora nor cups."

"I know just the thing." Perseus walked

away, heading toward the water. "Stay with him."

"But I . . ." Ammon went quiet, looked up at the powerful animal. Nervously, he patted the white neck. It was like patting an anvil.

"Now then, don't fret, don't fret, my bird-like friend. Your master will be back in a moment. You don't frighten me, you know. You're only a horse, even if you can fly, even if you are gifted by the gods, even if you could trample me to a small, wet pulp under your hooves. No, you don't frighten me. Like Hades you don't.

"I should have brought an apple for you. Or maybe a pine cone. But I can't think of everything, can I? I'm only a poor old playwright. Be good, and I'll write you a sonnet some day."

The stallion reared slightly and whinnied. Ammon stayed close, tried to speak reassuringly. It was difficult, however, considering the quaver in his voice.

"Be good now, great Pegasus, master of the sky. Perhaps you'd prefer a whole play, eh?" He looked anxiously toward the water. What was that boy up to, and what was keeping him?

"Here it is!" came the call from the shoreline a moment later. Perseus's outline bent, his actions concealed by darkness. Then he was returning, something shiny cupped in both hands. Pegasus gave the distracted poet a friendly nudge and sent him stumbling. Ammon kept his instinctive response to himself, however.

Perseus held out the helmet of Athene, now brimming with fresh water. The horse eyed him for a moment, then sniffed at the helmet. And then he was drinking in long, noisy gulps.

"Ah, so you grew thirsty too, my fine friend." Perseus said as he stroked the muzzle with one hand.

By the time the stallion finished, there was only a little left in the helmet. Symbolically, Perseus finished it, then caressed the horse affectionately.

"You and me from now on, my friend without feathers. We drink the same water. Even our names are similar. Perhaps we are related, eh?" He grinned at Ammon.

"We did it, old man. We've tamed the one steed in all the world fit for a god to ride."

Ammon shook his head and spoke admiringly. "No, my boy. *You* did it." He raised a hand to still Perseus's protest. "I was amply rewarded by being privileged to watch. I will derive a most wonderful play from this night. That is pleasure enough for me."

Perseus held the helmet right-side-up, let it drip clean. "What now? I have a few poor skills, my good friend, but little knowledge."

The mood surrounding them turned somber. "When it comes to tracking gigantic vultures who carry off the astral shells of sleeping princesses, I am as poorly experienced as you,

Perseus. We must plan carefully what you are to do next, for if it is truly Calibos who is behind these ghostly excursions of her spirit, only the wise and cautious may return to attest to it." He put a hand on Perseus's shoulder.

"I have grown fond of you in a short time, Perseus. And I even find myself feeling compassion for the Princess Andromeda, though I never thought I could feel sympathy for any member of royalty. I do not wish to see either of you become food for worms.

VI

Andromeda tossed spasmodically on the curtained bed. Always the same dream. Always the same, always frightening, but somehow compelling. Yet it seemed no matter how hard she tried to scream, she could never wake herself up.

It was coming for her again, as it had so many nights previously. How could she tell it was night or day, fast asleep as she was? The small part of her consciousness that remained did not know. What it did know was that it would have to watch helplessly as that true part of her was drawn off, sucked away by some horrid compulsion she was unable to resist. She was weak now, so weak from the repeated draining of self that if it continued much longer she was certain she would die.

She no longer feared death, however. It

was preferable to this unclean use of her inner self. Death would end the dreams and free her. A false freedom, she knew, but the only kind she could any longer look forward to.

Her body twisted and she cried out. Something was wrenching at her heart and mind, sending a shiver through her whole body. The magic that compelled her was urgent and brutal, content to have its way without regard for how it left her. She slumped once more, completely worn out, and devoid of hope.

Her second self rose and trod the path it had learned many times over. Down the marble dais, out through the archway, onto the balcony. The cage of gold awaited her there. Moist pools of crimson regarded her impatiently as she entered the open portal. The bars closed tight and she convulsively gripped the arms of her chair.

The vulture lifted from the balustrade. Once more it hovered, grasped the perch welded to the crest of the cage. It lifted ponderously into the night sky and soared to the northeast, retracing the same invisible path it had followed in coming. Nothing was changed, nothing was different.

Only one thing, perhaps.

This night, it had company.

High above and behind the bird, who was as easy to track on the cloudless night as a merchantman's dhow in an empty harbor, flew a far smaller, more agile shape. It was pale white and something dark sat on its back.

Perseus clung to the makeshift harness and kept his attention on the distant but still clearly defined silhouette of the vulture. The helmet and sword were secured to his belt. Ammon had urged him to take the shield also, but Perseus had declined, reasoning that its additional weight might reduce Pegasus's mobility.

"Besides," he'd told the poet, "if a sword that can slice through marble, and a helmet that renders its wearer invisible are not sufficient protection for one man, then I am unworthy to be husband to Andromeda."

Ammon had shaken a rueful finger at him in parting. "May your success match your gallantry, young Perseus, and not mark you an overconfident fool."

But the shield *was* heavy. Maybe the boy was right. Anyway, who was he to argue with him? He was a tired old writer, not a retired general. Marshal your words, Ammon, and let younger men marshal their weapons.

But damn, he'd thought as he'd watched man and horse soar upward into the night: I wish I were going with him.

The vulture continued to gain altitude, rising with mighty beats of its enormous wings. Perseus urged the stallion higher, hoping to remain far from the great bird's notice. It seemed intent only on carrying out its task of conveying the princess to some unknown destination, however, and paid no attention to the flocks of terrified birds it occasionally scattered.

A glance downward showed the towers and compounds of Joppa, lines of limestone and marble marring the earth. Behind him was the gleam of moonlight on the Mediterranean.

Perseus returned his attention forward, squinting into the wind and grateful that the night was not stormy. He'd spent too much time in too many small boats out on the ocean for the dips and rises of the flying horse to make him sick. But his mind was filled with too many other thoughts and worries for him to enjoy the spectacular ride.

Finally the vulture began descending toward a layer of low clouds. Perseus urged the horse to a faster pace, not wanting to lose sight of his quarry.

I've been asleep, he thought with amazement. Thank the gods I did not fall!

He roused himself to full alertness, watching the huge carrion-eater sink into a shifting, cloying mist. They were far from the cool shore breezes of Joppa now. The air rising from below was humid and hot. Where moisture met desert in the lowlands and where there was ample ground water, one sometimes found the foulest of swamps. It was a fitting home for the vulture.

And for its master, Perseus thought darkly. He dug his thighs into Pegasus's flanks, murmuring "Down." Soon they too were swallowed up by the mists.

As they dropped, the temperature began to rise. Soon it was uncomfortably humid, despite the fact that it had been a pleasant night in Joppa. Sweat rolled from both man and horse. Perseus peered downward but could see nothing, and had to hope his mount had a better sense of its surroundings than did its poor, blinded rider.

Then the mist seemed to lighten, letting the moonlight through, and he could see they were not far from the surface.

The trees of the benighted land were twisted as if in pain, their leaves hungry for the sunlight that rarely penetrated here. Bushes crouched low to the earth, as though ashamed of what this land had made them. There were no flowers. Even the reeds and rushes looked unhealthy, marked as they were by gray, scabrous growths that clung persistently to their stems.

Water moved like oil, sluggish and tired. In places noisome smells rose from bubbling pits of sludge. From time to time something hiding deep in this foul landscape would emit a challenging, lingering cry, a sound as devoid of beauty or grace as its surroundings.

Somewhere in that mist was a huge disturbance where something large moved. Feet followed cage as the vulture descended to the rheumy earth. It hovered carefully and let the golden prison settle easily onto a sandbar flanking what passed in that land for a flowing stream.

The door opened. The figure of Andromeda rose mechanically and stepped out. She began walking toward a dark, gaping hole in the mossy flank of a crumbling cliff. Cawing approvingly to itself, the vulture settled nearby on a massive exposed root the thickness of many trees. Its eyes closed. It would wait thus until summoned.

No normal young woman, no matter how brave, would stride so indifferently through that nightmare landscape. Toads and beetles the size of dogs crossed her path, scuttling or hopping out of her way. She ignored them, oblivious to their presence. A crocodile slid through the brackish water nearby, a lean, dark, green length of solid muscle. It edged in its loglike fashion closer and closer to the walking figure.

Then it took note of something unseen. The reptilian eyes could not show fear, but the carnivore turned instantly from its intended prey and dove with a violent slash of its powerful tail, leaving only a trail of bubbles in its wake.

There was a sound of footsteps and breaking twigs. The feet that made imprints on the soft earth were no longer entirely human. Once they were. Now they supported a demonic grotesquerie. Anger and magic had turned that powerful figure into something out of delirium. Its posture was crooked, the face a twisted mask of failed humanity, a true mirror of the mind that now lay buried beneath horn and bone.

It could not wait any longer within its lair and so had lurched out to meet Andromeda. She stopped. The silence that ensued was broken only by the sounds of bubbles bursting in the muck, by an excited cry from the briefly awakened vulture, and by a persistent, unpleasant, heavy breathing.

Two massive arms reached for the slightly swaying figure of the princess. They held the ends of a necklace of fine gold worked by the inhuman smiths who inhabit the border region between Earth and Hades.

"A gift for you," the figure growled thickly. Andromeda did not react. Her eyes stared vacantly forward, as though the gift-giver were not present.

Calibos placed the necklace around her throat, his hands trembling slightly at the nearness. Thick fingertips wrestled with the latch and finally succeeded in securing it. Then the man-thing stepped back, studying the effect of the necklace on that smooth, pale throat. It shone brightly even in the dim misty light, testimony to the skill of goldsmiths who worked with things finer than hands.

"It is good. It becomes you, Andromeda. Your neck flatters the gold." She did not respond.

He grunted hoarsely and turned to gesture imperiously toward the dark hollow in the cliff face. Obediently Andromeda resumed her walk, the beast following impatiently. He limped slightly on his cloven hoof, favoring the still human foot.

Once the place might have been a temple. Now it offered shelter only to creatures of the dark, to persistent probing roots and plants. Water dripped from the roof of crumbling limestone. The place had witnessed war and pestilence in eons past. Now it was to Calibos his refuge, to anyone else, his lair.

Skulls decorated portions of the cavern, their bleached curves whiter than the decaying marble they were perched upon. There were weapons taken from those foolish enough to cross into Calibos's domain, each spear or sword set by a matching skull.

Andromeda walked in, impassively moving past ruined blocks of stone which had tumbled to the floor, stepping over cracks and crevices. She knew what was expected of her. She halted before the ancient throne which Calibos had made his own. Silent and helpless, she stood there and waited.

Calibos marched up beside her, hesitated a moment as always, then ascended his throne. He sat silently studying her, one clawed hand tapping an arm of his seat. It was quiet in the cavern. As before, they had a waiting game to play out.

And as before, it was Andromeda who broke the silence and spoke first. If she did not, Calibos would remain content simply to drink in the sight of her. It was easier to have him talking.

"Calibos . . . why have you summoned me here, yet again? Why so many journeys, so many times? I've never before asked you your reasons."

"Is that because you feared to know the answer?" he countered. "Or can it be that your curiosity has finally overcome your fears?"

"I think I have always known, but saw no reason to discuss the inevitable. You know that I will not marry you. Your magic compels me to come here, but not all the power of the dark spirits can force me to accept you."

"Little fool." He shook his head slowly, his expression a cross between smile and snarl, the two welded together by frustration.

"I know that as well as you. Did you think, though, that I would surrender you so easily? I cannot have you, but even if I cannot look on your true beauty, I can bring its mirror image here, and look on it, and remember how you once loved me. And I will continue to do so until we are both aged and deformed." He laughed at his own humor, a deep, guttural noise.

"Loved? I was promised to you, Calibos. Promised as an infant. I never loved you, not then and not now. Once I respected you as a noble lord, but even that soon left me."

"*You loved me!*" A heavy fist slammed down on the arm of the throne, nearly crackling the wood. The sound reverberated through the cavern. Tiny crawling things rushed for deeper, safer holes. "You did!"

"No, Calibos. Never."

"You did, you did, you did! Before Zeus damned me, before I was cursed with deformity." He calmed himself and his tone softened.

"Remember how I was then, Andromeda." He spoke imploringly. "Remember what I was like as . . . as a man."

"I remember. You were handsome and strong. But the inner self your body now mimics showed through even then. You were cruel, Calibos. Cruel and callous and uncaring. You laughed at those who were not blessed with your heritage, your looks, your wealth, and you tormented those lesser than you.

"Now you have become less than them." She nodded once, sleepily. "This is not damnation you suffer, but justice."

"You reject me, as always."

"I cannot love you, Calibos of the Marshes. Not now and not even if you were changed back to your former self. I have seen you as you are. You would always remain ugly to me, Calibos." She raised a shaky, unsteady hand and pointed at him. "You see, Calibos, I know you."

The Lord of the Marshes turned his head away as if in pain. In his anguish he could not tell for certain whether it was his unrequited love or the truth of Andromeda's words which stung him more.

Then he whirled back round to glare down at her, nostrils flared, saliva dripping from the two fangs which had grown from his canines. His tone changed and his real self surged to the fore.

"Know then," he said harshly, his voice now a rasping probe, "that it is time for you to learn another mystery, to memorize another question. By the powers given to me by invocation to Father Hades, by the strength of my curse and by the goddess my mother Thetis, I hold you still to your marriage contract. Another question for another suitor—when will one answer you aright? When will the curse be broken?

"I will answer for you. Never! You will learn new questions and new riddles." He chuckled grossly, his true self taking free rein. "You will watch the worthy perish along with the pretenders. What pleasure you give to the executioners of Joppa! Never have they been so busy."

"No, I beg you. No more fires in the city square. No more deaths on my behalf."

"On your behalf? Why dearest Andromeda, sweetest Andromeda, Andromeda of the legendary beauty, it is not I who compel so many brave young men to join their predecessors at the stake. They do so voluntarily." He sneered down at her. "For the love of the fair princess.

"But in the end they all burn, and in so doing they have the better of me, for their passion is put to an end quickly, while mine curses me anew every day and night! Put an end to it? Fulfill your contract with me."

"You know I cannot, Calibos."

"I know you *will* not." He rose and cracked the whip he kept always close at hand.

Several desiccated figures, more scarecrow

than substance, stepped out into the dim light before the throne. One carried a torch of flaming pitch-soaked wood. A second held a flayed animal skin cured dry and tough as old parchment.

The third was dressed in the guise of a huntsman, which he might once have been. Now he served darker desires than mere hunger. From his right hand dangled the feathered leg and claw of a raven. The stump of the leg was ragged and torn. It had not been cut from its owner. Blood dripped steadily to the floor.

The three figures surrounded the motionless princess. She swayed, sickened as always by their nearness, but as always her legs would not obey her. Indeed, her legs were back in Joppa, sprawled asleep on the tower bed.

One of the scarecrow creatures unrolled the animal skin. Calibos leaned close, enjoying Andromeda's inability to draw away from his leprous visage.

"Look closely at the skin. Look! I command it." Reluctantly the princess's gaze dipped to examine the skin.

"Mark the words well, Andromeda. A new question to test the next would-be hero, a new puzzle for your next savior." Again the deep-throated chuckle sounded. "A new opportunity to warm the mob with the heat of burning flesh."

The huntsman-thing stepped forward and scrawled on the dry skin with the bloody claw. He drew a pair of circles, the smaller above the larger. Then he surrounded the circles with formal Greek, the calligraphy as crude as it was gory.

The huntsman worked hard and conscientiously, knowing too well the penalty for a smeared word or wrong letter. At last he was finished. Taking the skin from the figure holding it, he turned and held it so that Andromeda could see nothing else.

"Mark," the huntsman-thing commanded, "and remember-r-r-r-r." The voice was weak. The dead speak but infrequently, and so forget how to use their throats and tongues.

Andromeda stared at the skin, at the bloody symbol of Calibos's ring and the letters that danced mockingly around it. She could not turn away. Her eyes obeyed her no better than her legs.

The letters and their meaning were burnt into her brain, along with a reminder of the curse and its awful potential. She could not chance disobeying it, could not expose her own people. She would have to obey. In his wrath Zeus had inadvertently punished her as thoroughly as he had Calibos.

"You understand?" he asked her as the huntsman rolled up the skin. She nodded slowly.

"When the times comes, when the next suitor presents himself, you will remember the question you have just seen. Only the correct answer can free you," he said, smirking, "and send you into the arms of your lover. While he still has arms, that is." He turned his attention back to the servitors, who waited with the patience of the undead.

"Enough. Finish it."

The huntsman bowed slightly. Turning to the torchbearer, he thrust the rolled skin into the flames. The dry skin burned rapidly, producing a stench that affected even the Lord of the Marsh.

When only ashes remained of the skin and the new secret was safely sealed, the huntsman and his two necrotic companions turned and marched solemnly back into the shadows from whence they'd been called.

It was time to end another visit, Calibos mused. Time to let her return. He could keep her with him, he knew. Keep her here close and warm by him. But it was only her shade, her shadow, a part of her.

He wanted *all* of her.

It was promised that it should be so, he muttered to himself. No matter what she or anyone else says, it was promised. My curse keeps a tether on that promise, and I will hold fast to it forever. She *will* consent one day. Or she will grow old and die alone. Alone save for that part of her which I command.

He reached out and down, and with his hand touched the bare white shoulder. A single ring gleamed on one clawed finger as it moved down her arm. The circlet of silver was finely worked and topped by an enormous twin pearl. Calibos was not particularly fond of pearls but he fancied these because so many others envied him them and could not enjoy them while they remained in his possession.

Like Andromeda, he thought with satisfaction.

The claw hand traveled down the motionless arm, moved across the arch of one hip and down a lightly clad thigh. It lingered there.

"Calibos." Her voice had grown weaker and he knew he had to let her return. His hand tingled from the contact with her skin, secondhand or not.

"I implore you," she continued feebly. "I beg now as I have begged before. Lift your curse from Joppa and release my soul. Show pity, Calibos. You say you loved me and love me still. If that is so, then you will release me now."

Hesitantly the shade reached out to touch his cheek. He spent a long moment savoring the unexpected caress. Then in an instant, his twisted mind saw the touch as a lie, designed only to trick him. It was contempt she was showing him, not concern.

Well, he would have none of it, none! Did she think him so easily fooled?

Contemptuously he slapped her hand aside. "I do not want your pity, Andromeda. Beg all you please. I will continue to call out your soul as often as I like. I will release you from the curse only after you've agreed to fulfill your contract.

"Now go, get out, back to your sleeping shell, back in your precious city! I feel your

disgust for me even in your shade. Leave me
... and take with you the question for your
next panting suitor." He gestured angrily toward the opening leading out of the cavern and
turned away from her.

Andromeda's head dropped. It was not a
gesture born of despair or defeat. She was looking at the necklace he'd placed on her when
she'd first arrived.

Her fingers moved slowly, but insistently.
The latch opened, and with a slight splattering
sound the necklace fell into the mud at her
feet.

She turned and flowed toward the mouth of
the cave.

Calibos turned back, unable to deny himself the pleasure of watching her depart. He
stared fixedly at the grace and bearing of her
walk, the smooth movement of her legs and
hips. Outside, the vulture was beginning to
caw in expectation, preparatory to returning
the princess to her true body in distant Joppa.

Too much beauty, Calibos thought furiously. Too much so near, and yet never to be his.
Unable to look at her any longer he turned his
gaze downward.

Even the necklace had been spurned because it came from him. The necklace which he
had bargained for at the border of Hades itself.
It lay like a strand of ordinary beads half buried in the moist earth, discarded and shut out
as callously as his love and ...

His eyes flickered and he leaned sharply

forward, like a cat mindful of the sudden, unexpected proximity of prey. The necklace lay ignored where Andromeda had dropped it, half glittering in the slime.

Whence arise these oddly familiar depressions close by the strand of gold? he thought.

Strange—too small to be his own and the princess's shade left none. There were many of them, and even as he stared, more of them appeared. They were moving toward the cavern entrance, following in the princess's wake.

How intriguing—more magic than his own was apparently at work this night. It promised a diversion most welcome to one whose principal pastime was bemoaning his unfortunate fate.

Calibos hopped off the throne, crouching low over the ground, and slowly started to follow the alien footprints.

Scarecrows and large newts, skeletons and half-rancid corpses—the attendants of Calibos's dark court moved to join him to see what had attracted his attention. He snapped his whip once and they shrank back, crawling into their holes and crevices.

The footprints followed the princess's path until well outside the cavern. Then they turned to one side. Calibos followed them expectantly.

It was still night in the swamps, but somehow the moon penetrated the mists enough to illuminate the grotesque terrain. Will-o'-the-wisps danced among the creepers and owls hooted dispiritedly as they searched for rodents. The frogs and toads were in full voice, their croaking rising in a crescendo that would climax with the dawn.

Perseus struggled through the muck. His sword was still fastened securely at his belt, but he'd nearly lost the helmet twice already because of poor footing. If the helmet fell into some bottomless mud sump it would be lost to him forever. Confident now in the success of his journey, he removed it and tucked it securely under one arm.

His gaze went upward, though there was very little difference between mist and sky.

"Pegasus!" he called out as loudly as he dared, though he estimated he'd come a considerable distance from Calibos's lair. He continued wading through the fog. "Pegasus, my good friend! To me!"

Where had the stallion taken himself? If he'd lost interest in his recently acquired human companion and had flown off, it would be a long journey indeed back to far Joppa.

"Come, Pegasus!"

A frog sprang alertly out of his path, landing with a splash in the dark water. Perseus made his way around a massive dead stump whose exposed roots were thicker around than a man.

He examined the broken top. Perhaps his voice would carry better from higher up, and he might be able to gain some idea of his immediate surroundings. He did not recall passing the stump, but surely he'd left the flying horse lightly tethered somewhere nearby.

The roots of the ancient stump were twisted like brown wire. Perseus moved to the base, seeking a suitable route upward. He was an excellent climber and the stump was not that high.

Several roots were too small, others too rotted to support his weight. Since his attention was directed upward, he failed to notice the slight movement of two of the smaller roots. One of them displayed a pair of shining blobs near its end. Closer inspection would have revealed what might be unusually large pearls.

"Pegas-u-u-us! To me, friend!"

He paused a moment to ready himself for the short climb. Behind him, roots that were not roots moved with astonishing speed, wrapping hard around his neck. At the youth's imprisoned throat the pearls gleamed sickly in the wan moonlight.

Instinctively, Perseus jabbed backward with an elbow. He hit something as solid as the logs he'd passed. The figure holding him laughed—a taunting, inhuman sound. He jabbed again and met unyielding flesh.

Around his neck the single hirsute arm was contracting like a snake. It tightened slowly, as if to prolong the motion, to hurt as well as kill.

Perseus struck lower. There was a grunt of surprise and the arm around his burning throat relaxed. Perseus spun free, but as he did so the helmet tumbled from his grasp. He had no time to hunt for it, Calibos had recovered and was reaching to renew the fatal embrace.

The monster was surprisingly agile, but few were as supple and quick as Perseus. Avoiding the powerful fingers that sought his throat, he struck repeatedly at the broad body confronting him, searching for a weak point within the half-reptilian flesh.

While they fought, the helmet of invisibility rolled down the slight embankment to disappear forever, claimed like so many artifacts and men by the clinging muck of the swamp.

Only Perseus's speed kept him from being overpowered. But the terrain worked to his disadvantage, slowing him down and finally allowing the more ponderous Calibos to gain a second grip on him. Down they went into the mud, with the grinning Calibos on top, forcing the youth back and down toward the waiting water.

Somehow Perseus got his sword free. But for all his inhuman appearance, Calibos was no blind, raging animal. Seeing the danger immediately, he slapped one hand on Perseus's wrist, pinning it and the sword harmlessly against the earth while the other hand continued to force the youth's head back toward the mud.

VII

Of all the structures financed by the commerce of Phoenicia, none was more elaborate or beautiful than the great temple of the city of Joppa. Though smaller, it boasted more columns of rich marble and finer tapestries than the Parthenon in distant Athens. Its ceiling was higher, its appointments more luxurious. There was even a second-floor balcony which gave it an intimacy many smaller buildings might have envied.

At the far north end of the temple rose a great marble statue of Thetis, patron goddess of the city. Gold and ivory decorated the goddess's likeness. She sat on a marble throne of seashells and creatures of the sea, her back supported by the graceful, arching shape of a seahorse. Silken canopies of the richest purple shielded her from above. Her immovable form frozenly gazed down at those who might come to worship, to beg favors or forgiveness.

This morning the temple was crowded. The usual ceremonies had been performed to assuage the privileged, the priests had done obeisance and executed their sacrifices, had delivered their sermons and ran through their genuflections.

A smattering of ordinary citizens pushed and shoved among the wealthy—those fortunate enough to have some pull with this or that official or merchant or soldier of the guard. They anxiously awaited the next act of the continuing drama which kept the city beneath a permanent cloud of doom.

There was a brassy, flat blare of trumpets and a stampeding roll of drums. Queen Cassiopeia appeared, followed by the slow-moving, completely veiled form of the princess.

They halted next to the foot of the statue. The fanfare died. Cassiopeia surveyed the crowd from where she stood, ringed by the lanky shapes of the temple priests. Separating them from the crowd was a line of soldiers, alert now that some important duty was demanded of them.

Even old Thallo's armor was polished to a high shine, his leather oiled and supple. He and his companions were all business now.

The milling throng hushed as all turned expectantly toward the dais fronting the statue.

"Once again," a silvery, strong voice announced to them, "I, Cassiopeia, Queen of Joppa, present to you my daughter Andromeda. If there be any man here worthy to seek her hand in marriage, then let him now make himself known to us." Her lips closed tight, completing her grim expression.

"All know the conditions which must be met before such a proposal may meet with acceptance," she continued. "Let a worthy suitor step forth!"

There followed the usual uncomfortable shuffling by the citizenry, and an embarrassing silence.

"Come, come," the queen finally urged, "is there no one? No man worthy in all the wide Kingdom of Phoenicia? No man of courage in all the world?" The silence was total, save for sandals scuffing marble.

The queen's gaze roved over the crowd. "You there—charioteer near the back. I mark you by your color and countenance as a man of Aegypt. Would not a son of the Nile like to be King of Phoenicia?"

"Not, I, good Queen!" the man replied, his speech marked by the accent of his southerly homeland.

Her eyes moved to the right. "Numidian," she said, speaking to a tall dark mercenary leaning against a column, "they say the fighting men of Africa are the bravest in the world, that they feast regularly on lions and crocodiles to keep their strength up and do battle with the lightning of Zeus himself. Would you not take the Princess of Joppa to wife?"

"Forgive me, great Queen," replied the ebony warrior in a clear voice, his leopard's skull shifting on his head, "but far rather would I battle the lightning. I have not been so short a time in Joppa that I am ignorant of the 'conditions' of which you speak."

There was a rustle of uncomfortable laughter from the crowd. A sharp glance from Cassiopeia silenced it as if by a sword.

"Where is another man of courage?" she demanded loudly, almost desperately. "Where is he who will rescue my daughter from this curse?" Again the empty response.

"Cowards!" she shouted. "I am the ruler of a city of cowards!"

"But not of fools," said a soft voice somewhere in the bowels of the crowd.

"Where is the man who spoke just then?" Cassiopeia's eyes narrowed as she hunted for the jester. "Let him come up here and joke about this to my face." The crowd became as still as the Pillars of Hercules.

In that absence of sound and movement, the creaking as the temple doors were moved aside startled everyone. Those near the back of the temple turned first and the movement flowed through the crowd like a wave, the tactless jester instantly forgotten.

The tall doors had been parted just

enough to admit a man. He stumbled a little; his body was bruised, his face bloody. His clothing, where intact, was thick with mud and grime. From both shoulders hung a royal cloak trimmed with gold. Experienced merchants in the crowd immediately noted that the gold was fake. The bruises and cuts on his body were real, however, and not the product of clever makeup.

Trotting in behind him with immense dignity was the stubby form of a playwright and poet recognized by only a few startled members of the crowd.

There was something in the young man's appearance and manner which made the crowd part instinctively to let him through. Or perhaps it was the ferocity of his gaze.

As he marched unchallenged toward the base of the statue of Thetis, he struggled to straighten, to cure himself through sheer willpower of the injury which was causing him to limp.

At the first steps he stopped, looking hard at those waiting there, and then lifted an arm in salute to the queen. The soldiers regarded him uncertainly. They eyed their officers and awaited instructions, while the officers in turn waited for a command from the queen.

Cassiopeia was alternately amused and impressed by the young stranger. Anyone with the audacity to interrupt such an important ceremony was worthy of attention. She took note of his fresh wounds, his overall appearance, the ragtag attire that was half beggar and half king.

"Who might you be, my cocky young visitor?"

"I am Perseus. Prince Perseus, if you please, lady." He drew himself up.

"Prince Perseus indeed." She did not smile. "Prince of mud and delusion, it would seem."

"Prince and heir to the Kingdom of Argos, such as it may be."

Mention of that ill-fated city across the sea raised a curious murmur from the assembly.

Cassiopeia was not impressed. "Really? And what do you wish of us, Prince Perseus of Argos-such-as-it-may-be?"

He turned to face the princess, who did not react to his presence. She began to show signs of curiosity, however, if not recognition.

"I know the penalty and the rewards."

"Penalty and . . ." Cassiopeia's attitude toward the bedraggled figure changed radically. She tempered her delight with caution. "Know what you are about, young man. This is no puppet show here, put on to amuse bored children. Think on what you are about to do."

He looked back up at her. "Death by burning if I fail; marriage to Andromeda if I succeed."

"I see that you have thought on it. Then it shall be as you wish, young man." She looked to one side and raised an arm commandingly.

The drums and gongs of the temple musicians commenced a steady drone, above which rose the excited buzzing of the crowd. The story of Argos and its destruction was known to most, and was quickly shared with the ignorant. Many believed the tale, but the ancestry of this stranger who claimed to be its long-lost prince was clearly open to question.

Not that it mattered. Gallant he surely was; prince he might or might not be; but he would most certainly smoke and scream as readily as the others when the fire licked at his ankles. That was the consensus of the crowd. There was not even any betting, as had sometimes happened on such occasions. The odds had long since proven themselves too one-sided.

Gently, the queen raised the veil from Andromeda's face. She lifted her eyes uncertainly, and when her gaze found that of her latest suitor, her confusion was magnified. She blinked and shook her head as if to clear it, then stared harder at the young man. He returned her stare with equal fervor.

"I . . . I am still asleep," she finally muttered dazedly. "You . . . ? You are not real."

Cassiopeia had thought the day's surprises at an end. Now her gaze bounced back and forth between her daughter and this self-annointed prince.

"You know him?"

Andromeda swayed, tried to keep her balance. Her reply came as if from a distance: "Only from a dream."

She looked down into Perseus's eyes, fighting to remember ... what? Surely they had been staring deeply into her own not long ago. Was she then to be haunted by day now as well as by night?

"I ... whoever you are, sir, you seem a kindly man," she told him. "I would not see you perish like the others. I beg you, for your own safety, abandon any thoughts you may have about me." But she spoke without conviction and continued to stare bewilderedly down at him.

Perseus answered with all the confidence she lacked. "Do not fear for me, Princess. I know well the conditions. Ask your riddle."

"I would rather—" She stopped in mid-sentence and sighed deeply. No matter how she tried she could not break the compulsion imposed upon her. She closed her eyes and her voice took on the ethereal quality of her astral double. Her words came like a distant incantation:

"This then is the riddle, bold stranger. In my mind's eye I see three circles joined in priceless, graceful harmony. Two full as the moon, one hollow as a crown. Two from the sea, five fathoms down. One from the Earth deep under the ground.

"The whole a mark of high renown. Tell me, what can it possibly be?"

The temple had become utterly quiet.

Vengeful Zeus (Sir Laurence Olivier) orders the destruction of the city of Argos for abandoning to the sea the mother Danae and her child Perseus.

Perseus (Harry Hamlin), the mortal son of Zeus, is transported by heavenly powers to the city of Joppa to meet his destiny.

With the help of Ammon (Burgess Meredith), a Greek playwright, Perseus is able to capture the great flying horse Pegasus.

Princess Andromeda (Judi Bowker) is threatened by the evil Calibos with whom Perseus must do battle in his swamp lair.

Perseus, Ammon, Andromeda, and soldiers set out to save the city of Joppa from the Kraken.

They are aided by the goddess Athene (Susan Fleetwood) who sends them the mechanical owl Bubo to help them gain information from the three Stygian witches.

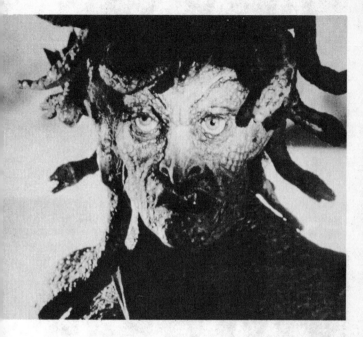

The object of their quest and their only weapon against the Kraken—the head of the Gorgon.

Perseus is forced to do battle against the Forest Scorpions.
Perseus and Andromeda are finally reunited without fear.

Even the insects outside seemed frightened into silence. Andromeda opened her eyes and stared with forlorn hopelessness at the handsome young stranger.

"Have courage, Princess." He tapped one cheek with a finger and appeared almost to be mocking the question. "Now, what can it be? Three circles joined, two moons and a crown?"

"*Tell* me," she pleaded, almost daring to hope again, as she had hoped so many futile times before.

"Have a care, stranger," Cassiopeia advised him. "You toy with your very life."

Perseus did not turn his gaze from the princess. "The answer is . . . a ring. A ring formed of two joined pearls on a circle of gold!"

He threw open a flap of his cloak and held something aloft. It was a hand, the severed end cut cleanly at the wrist and dark with dried blood. Light flashed from the index finger.

"The ring of the Lord of the Marsh—the pearl ring of Calibos, here on the claw hand of Calibos himself."

He threw the grisly trophy to the floor. It slid across the smooth marble to stop abruptly at the foot of the statue of Thetis.

"The ring. A present from his mother, the goddess Thetis. Is that not truly the right answer to the question?"

Andromeda did not reply. Her head was in her hands and she was sobbing uncontrollably. Nearby stood the dumbfounded Cassiopeia, her eyes moving from the ghastly disembodied hand to her daughter.

"Tell me, is it?" Perseus pressed her.

Finally the princess regained just enough control of her emotions to gasp out, "Yes, yes!" over her weeping.

The silence in the temple lingered a moment longer before it was shattered like crystal by a mighty roar from the crowd.

Ah, the feelings that overcame the assembly at that moment! Such a scene had not occurred in Joppa since its founding. All the tension, all the fears that had enveloped the city during the past months evaporated. Enemies hugged one another, and husbands and wives fell into each other's arms in ecstasy. Even the soldiers momentarily forgot themselves, breaking position to congratulate their comrades.

After all, 'tis not everyday that a curse is lifted from a whole city.

As the noise began to fade, Perseus lifted his own voice to make himself heard above it. "We fought in the swamp," he shouted to the enthralled crowd. "Battled on his own ground. I spared his life on one condition: that he renounce his curse, which he did. There will be no more bonfires in the city square, no more nightmares. No more young men need volunteer their lives.

"You are freed. Joppa is free." He turned back to the princess, who was staring at him with a mixture of wonder and delight, and said more softly, "And you are free, Andromeda.

Only I am not, for I am captured by your beauty and bound by your love." His eyes dropped.

"I know that I have won you, by the terms of the curse and by the binding your mother the queen placed upon it. But I have won only a title." He looked into her face, smiled awkwardly.

"I ask—not demand—that you give me a chance to win also your heart."

She might not have fallen, but it was natural enough that he should be there to catch her as she slumped toward him. She clung to his willing support and gazed up into his eyes with an expression as hopeful as his own.

"I will gladly give that which you could take, Perseus. You have already won more than I thought I had left to give."

The cheers and shouts of the crowd had grown deafening. Cassiopeia beamed at the couple while nearby Ammon looked on approvingly. A fitting climax to the tale, he told himself, though perhaps a bit overly dramatic in its resolution. He would have added some comedy. But then, fate was a notoriously somber director.

Cassiopeia was equally pleased with the picture the two young lovers presented. Prince or not, this Perseus was as brave as any king. Comely and clever, and apparently truly in love with her daughter. A better match could not have made itself.

She was as happy as any of the common citizens currently dancing in the temple. With the weight of the accursed Calibos off her shoulders, she could again devote her energies and talents to expanding the commerce and power of her city. Someday this Perseus would rule alongside her daughter, and she would leave to them not a kingdom but an empire, if the gods were willing.

Possibly some of them might be. But in that moment of unrestrained triumph, the priests failed to notice how the stone face of Thetis changed from one of a benign smile to a perceptible frown. . . .

The queen's personal apartments were spacious and decorated in a manner befitting the ruler of so wealthy and important a state. The chambers were overflowing with riches brought back from distant lands: amber from the Baltic, silver from the Balkan tribes, ivory from Africa.

The entertainment was sparse but sophisticated. Cassiopeia was not one to open the royal coffers recklessly. A lone flute player and another man with a lyre alternately whistled and plucked a delicate tune to which a single dancer spun for the delectation of the assembly. But the musicians and the dancer were the best in all Joppa, and the audience watched them admiringly.

Ammon sat near the queen. Thallo stood behind them, a position of considerable honor. Ordinarily he would have been nervous at being assigned so critical a post, but this night even the royal guard was relaxed. This time it was the curse and not another brave young suitor that had perished.

Off to one side sat Perseus, holding hands with Andromeda. They whispered and laughed quietly and might as well have been in a boat out at sea for all the attention they paid to the entertainment. They had discovered far finer pleasures in each other's eyes.

"A fine couple," the queen observed with satisfaction. "This Perseus has the bearing of a king if not yet the wisdom. Some day he will be a worthy ruler. As for my daughter, I have not seen her so content and happy since she was a child. I still tend to see her as that from time to time." She sighed. "Soon I must give that up forever."

"Yes, a splendid pair, Majesty," agreed Ammon. "But young and hot-blooded. I think this dancing,"—he gestured at the performers —"not much to their liking."

"They'll have to be patient." Cassiopeia remembered whom she was talking to and assumed a slightly more regal tone. "The amenities must be observed. This is a royal wedding. Surely tomorrow at midday is soon enough. I would send off my only child according to custom."

"You look more like sisters, Majesty." Ammon risked a quick wink.

"Flatterer. I would be more receptive to your compliments if I did not know that you were primarily an author of comedies and farces."

"There is no humor in my compliments to you, Majesty. Only truth."

"You're a clever old fox, Ammon. I can see why Perseus favors you."

"Nay, Majesty, it is I who favor him. He would not be here this moment, holding hands with your daughter and preparing to marry her on the morrow, if not for my advice and aid."

"Or so you would have us all believe." But she smiled as she spoke.

"I have been the ruler of a city founded on commerce far too long to believe in the innocence of men, especially one as sharp-tongued and ingratiating as yourself. Tell me, what are you hoping to gain from all this?"

"Me?" Ammon looked properly outraged. "Majesty, you do me an injustice. What more could I want than for the city of Joppa, the home which I so dearly love, to recover its vigor and its former position as the center of trade, of experimentation—and of the arts?"

"Our trade endures, master of a hundred verbal convolutions, and we continue to experiment with life. As for the last, no doubt they will also experience a revival of interest, now that the people's minds have been lightened.

"Doubtless we will see new craftsmen in the marketplace, new people plying old trades ...and perhaps even the theater of comedy restored to its former elegance?"

Ammon shrugged, seemingly indifferent.

"It would not be bad for the people's spirits to taste a new comedy or two. As you say, they should be more receptive now."

Cassiopeia laughed, taking a sip of wine from a golden goblet. "We shall see. I am inclined to be generous toward public works now, for I have been given back my daughter." She eyed him across the rim of the goblet.

"And you, my supple-tongued friend—could it be that you just happen to have a new play ready to be staged?"

"Nay, Majesty," and before her surprised expression was lost he added quickly, "A dozen! And all brilliant. The wittiest Athenian writing today could not create more amusing soliloquies for Athens than I have for Joppa."

"As near as I can remember, your former works were quite popular with the masses, but sometimes of improper content. Certain authorities do not consider themselves fit subjects for buffoonery."

"But it is they who insist on lending themselves to parody, Majesty. And such amusements alleviate the worries and woes of the average man." He hastened to add, "These new plays I've written wouldn't offend anyone. All very proper, I assure you, dignified and moral."

"A pity."

"What is, Majesty?"

She grinned at him. "I rather liked the improper ones."

It was deserted in the temple.

A few torches still flickered from brackets set high in the walls. Several sandals, a brightly colored sash, other debris remained undisturbed where they'd been dropped and forgotten during the celebration earlier. Not even a priest was present. They were busily readying for the rituals of a royal marriage and had much to prepare.

A faint creaking sounded from the main entranceway, and a thin sliver of moonlight entered the torchlit chamber through the parted doors.

No guards stood ready to challenge. On so joyous a day it was unthinkable that anyone would try to desecrate the temple. The priests had declared that the doors should remain unlocked so that any who might wish to give private thanks for the deliverance of the princess would have free access to the temple at any hour.

The single figure that now hobbled into the temple was not there to give thanks. He had traveled a long way in considerable pain, and his body was flooded with rage, not thankfulness. Even had guards been present, they would not have been able to keep him outside.

His feet dragged tiredly across the marble floor. One arm ended not in fingers but in a bundle of stained, dirty bandages. He shuffled onward until he was standing at the base of the great statue. A last look around revealed that he was still alone within the sanctuary.

His eyes lifted to the face of the sculpture.

"Thetis, divine goddess of the sea, hear the prayer of thy son Calibos! Show me the way to justice. Show me how to punish the blasphemer Perseus, for such I have since learned is the name of he who did *this*!" and he thrust the bandaged, bloody stump toward the statue.

There was no reply, so he continued. "In wounding me, he has insulted you. Surely he must be punished. Help me. Show me what to do, and I will carry out your will."

A peculiar glow emerged from the face of the statue. The marble softened and flowed as though it had turned to soft clay beneath the hands of a master sculptor. When all the hardness had finally left the polished stone, the face of Thetis looked down expressionlessly.

"Perseus is protected by Zeus himself. There is nothing I can do."

"What of this insult to you? And what of this?" Again he waved the handless arm.

Thetis's voice was not cold, but neither was it promising. "A sharper than mortal sword cut off your hand, Calibos, but it was a mortal hand that wielded it. It was a fair fight. More than fair, I should say, for you have the strength of any two men."

"Even Hercules would have trouble defeating an eel."

The goddess did not sound impressed. "And even though you would have slain him in an instant, and tried to do so, still he spared your life. I do not call such an action blasphemy.

"Be grateful this lesson has cost you only a hand. I cannot act against Zeus's orders. I cannot punish this Perseus. You must fight your own fight, Calibos. You would involve Olympus in a private quarrel."

"Then if you cannot punish him, punish those he loves: the queen, Andromeda, the people of Joppa." He smiled, but there was no humanity or humor in it.

"How ironic it would be if the same fate that befell Argos happened here because of Perseus. A second such manifestation in his wake would cause him to be shunned in every city in the world. No country would offer him sanctuary for fear of suffering a similar fate." He glared sharply at the statue.

"Persuade your devoted Poseidon to let loose the Kraken against this city too. The god of the waters is brother to Zeus and would stand against him if you asked it. Let the Kraken destroy Joppa as it once destroyed Argos. I demand this justice!"

"Justice?" The voice of Thetis was soft, though it emerged from a stone throat. "Or revenge? I will consider the matter, but you displease me, Calibos. What grace and dignity you received from me has vanished. Perhaps it was gone even before Zeus saw reason to punish you."

The glow from above faded, and with it, Calibos's hopes. No priest appeared to see the half-human shape pounding in rage with its one remaining hand against the unyielding marble of the statue.

The dancers had given their best turns and highest leaps to the royal audience and had retired, but the musicians played on. Lute and lyre and flute formed a gentle background to conversation.

Perseus rose and led Andromeda from the audience chamber. No one noticed their subtle departure save old Ammon, who merely smiled a little wider and endeavored to draw the queen into deeper conversation.

A palace grows like a nautilus, adding newer and larger chambers as it matures. Such a method of expansion leaves small forgotten places here and there: hallways leading nowhere, rooms without ceilings, atriums that appear when least expected. Joppa's palace had a long way to go before it matched in extent and complexity such labyrinths as the Palace of Knossos in far-off Crete, but already there were places where lovers could conspire in peace.

In the half-light of the torches Perseus turned Andromeda toward him.

"I was getting tired of all the people, of all the questions. One more question about how

Argos came to be destroyed and I thought I would throw wine in someone's face. They all forget I was an infant at the time."

"But you are no infant now," she said coyly.

"Not for some time." He leaned toward her. To his surprise she hesitated, turned her lips aside.

"Why shouldn't we kiss?" he asked her. "At noon tomorrow you will become my wife." When Andromeda neither replied nor turned back to him, he grew puzzled.

"Isn't that what you want? To be my wife? For, by all the gods, I wish more than anything else on this earth to become your husband."

"It is agreed. You fought and defeated Calibos. You answered his riddle rightly. You won me."

"To have won you is not enough, as I said only hours ago. To be your husband is not enough, and I care nothing to be ruler of Joppa and Phoenicia. I don't understand, Andromeda. Do you not realize I care only that you love me?"

She faced him and her expression was tormented. "Love? I want that too, more than anything, but how can I be sure?"

"You were sure this morning."

"It was all so fast, so overpowering. Consider, Perseus, that I saw you for the first time in my life a few hours ago, streaked in blood and grime and waving a severed hand over your head."

He grinned. "A rapid and unorthodox courtship, I agree." Then he grew serious once more. "But I meant everything I said in the temple. This is meant to be. Don't you feel that also, Andromeda?"

"I . . . I think I do, but I want to be certain. I was first promised to Calibos. I want to want you willingly, not because you fought him or solved a riddle."

"Did you love Calibos? Is that what troubles you now?"

"Before he was changed, you mean? No. I am certain of that. There was never love. He was handsome and fascinating, and as a girl I tried to love him because it was promised that someday we would marry. But I never could. The evil that now shows in his face was there in his actions and words even as a child. I was very young, but I could still see."

"And now?"

"Now I feel pity for him. When you fought together in the swamps, why didn't you kill him? It would have been better."

"For us?"

"For him. You see, even while he has been tormenting me these past many months, I know how I must have been tormenting him. But I can feel no love. Only pity." She looked away again.

"There is still much that I do not understand. Everything has happened so fast, so fast. We met today and yet you said you have loved me longer."

"I have. I've seen you before today. I saw you in your sleep." He smiled tenderly. "You see the power you have over me, Andromeda. You conquered me even while asleep."

"Asleep? There was a dream, but surely that cannot have been real."

He put a finger to her lips. "It is said by wise men that what we see in dreams is truer than anything we see during our waking lives. That is the promise of Morpheus.

"When first I saw you, I thought I had set eyes on a dream myself, for surely, I thought, such beauty cannot exist in the waking world."

Her confusion cleared a little. "You say you are but a simple fisherman though of royal ancestry, yet you speak of love like one of Aphrodite's own courtiers."

He laughed softly and it echoed down the quiet corridor. "I have been forced for hours to listen to my friend Ammon. They say the talk of poets is catching, like a disease."

She smiled hesitantly back at him. "I think I find it a most pleasant infection."

"All will be explained tomorrow night. Then we will have each other only to ourselves and none can come between us. Simply believe me for now. Believe *in* me. I saw you asleep and the sight went through me like an arrow. I will wear that arrow forever." He held her tightly.

"From that first instant I was prepared to do anything for you. From that moment I loved you. Even the gods cannot explain the ways of love. Do you wish more proof than my poor words?"

"You defeated Calibos, risking your life not knowing how I would receive you. They say you tamed Pegasus himself simply so you could follow my shade to Calibos's lair. What further proof could I demand?"

He held up his right arm, stared into her eyes. "Ask me to cut off *my* hand and I'd do it!"

"No, no." She took his hand in both of hers, held it between her breasts. "I believe you. I believe you not because I am forced to, or because it is promised, but because I want to." She kissed the back of his hand. "I believe in you, Perseus. And in us."

"Enough to love me? Without questions?"

"Enough, but never without questions. I am the daughter of Cassiopeia of Joppa, Perseus. I am my mother's child. But the questions that I still have, have nothing to do with what truly matters."

"Which is?"

"That I believe now that I love you as much as you say you love me."

"Then show me."

She let his hand go and slowly put both arms around his neck, savoring the movement, the first contact. She kissed him gently at first, intending it to be no more than a first experimental exchange.

But experiments in affection have a way of

going astray, and when those who play are lovers, no control can restrain them. As Perseus said, even the gods cannot explain the ways of love. And if the gods cannot control themselves, then what can a man and a woman confronted with true passion do? One must feel a willingness, a desire to hold the other back, to fight it off.

Perseus and Andromeda did not wish to fight.

VIII

If the temple had been crowded the day before when the priests had been presiding over a possible sacrifice, it was jammed at the time set for the wedding. All of Joppa felt a part of the marriage. By answering the riddle Perseus had freed the princess. His marrying her assured the people their own freedom would be secured.

It had been a long time since the great temple had seen such lavish decoration. The atmosphere was as festive as on the days when returning ships unloaded the cargoes which made the city prosper.

The atmosphere in the temple was not that of royalty sharing with commoners but rather that of a single large family. Cassiopeia perceived this and was gratified beyond dreaming.

Her people were happy, and therefore so was she.

She stood at the base of Thetis's statue, resplendent in one of her richest gowns. All eyes were on her and the young couple standing patiently before her.

She raised a hand and the hundreds of people gathered in the chamber immediately fell silent.

Let Perseus and Andromeda find their happiness in each other's arms, she thought. The ability to command is my passion.

"Let all bear witness," she said, her voice ringing through the quiet room. "I, Cassiopeia of Joppa, Queen of Phoenicia, descendant of Pyrlos of Sidon, treaty-maker with the Empire of Persia, freely give my daughter and heir Andromeda in marriage to the noble Prince Perseus of Argos!"

She bent down and unfastened the ribbon symbolically girdling Andromeda's waist, then held it up for the crowd to see.

"As I link their wrists with this ribbon of silk, bear witness that as she is my heiress so Perseus becomes my male heir. As she is my daughter, so Perseus of Argos becomes my own son."

The betrothed held out their hands. Cassiopeia placed the ribbon across their wrists and prepared to pronounce the final blessing before gently knotting the cord.

Too much happiness can have the same effect as too much power. Both are akin to the effect produced from too much liquor. A pleasant, rosy haze dampens normal cautions, and the mind is inflamed to a point where a casual feeling of invulnerability overcomes the individual. It had happened to greater than Cassiopeia, and to lesser.

"I give her to the man who has rescued us all from despair," she continued, glorying in the joy of the moment, forgetful in the joy of the moment. "I give Andromeda, the most beautiful of all women, more beautiful than anything on Earth or in Heaven, more lovely even than . . ."

One of the priests, an attentive ascetic wedded to his duties, woke from a half sleep and started forward. There was a warning in his waving hands and an admonition forming on his lips, but both came too late to stop the queen.

". . . the goddess Thetis herself."

Perhaps only one thing is more terrible than the wrath of a god, and that is the jealousy of a beautiful woman. When the two are combined, even the laws and directives of Zeus himself are forgotten.

The entire temple—indeed, all of Joppa— quivered as though from an earthquake. It was accompanied, or perhaps initiated by, a cry of anger and outrage that came from no human throat.

The mood of the crowd changed swiftly from one of pleasant anticipation to one of terror. The elderly priest who might have rescued the moment froze in his tracks and knew without a doubt that he was too late.

Cassiopeia's thoughts screamed at her, overpowering her joy of a moment earlier and shaking her brutally back to reality. *Fool,* she thought in panic. *Fool of fools, queen of fools are you now!*

She turned as if in a dream to gaze up at the face of the great statue. Something within it cracked, and a darkness came over the city though the sun still shone brightly outside. It was an eclipse of the spirit.

Suddenly and yet slowly, the head of Thetis tumbled from the statue's neck. Cassiopeia, the priests, the soldiers of the guard and the two lovers scrambled aside as the four-foot head crashed to the dais. Splinters of marble spewed in all directions as the massive carving continued to bounce down to the floor of the temple.

Perseus grabbed the paralyzed Andromeda and tumbled with her to one side as another huge chunk of rock shattered down onto the spot where she'd been standing.

The marble head rolled slowly to a rest, and an instant of uncertain silence followed. Then the stone eyes flashed open and a more than mortal voice echoed through the room.

"Hear me, vain and foolish mortal woman! You *dare* to compare your daughter's beauty to mine, to one of the immortals? *In my own sanctuary!* You will regret your boast . . . and all will sorrow for the delight they feel over the cruel misfortune of my mortal son Calibos."

"Forgive me, Thetis! I did not mean—"

"In thirty days," the head continued relentlessly, "on the eve of the longest day of the year, your daughter Andromeda must be taken to the old sacrificial rock, where the first Canaanites paid homage to the gods of the sea who were so generous to them and their ungrateful offspring. There she must be bound and chained to the stone, a sacrifice to appease the anger of the sea goddess and to atone for your blasphemy—a sacrifice fit for the Kraken."

Few names could have rendered the crowd more terrified than they already were. That of the last of the Titans was one of them. Perseus held Andromeda protectively close, but there was no one to comfort the distraught Cassiopeia. She ruled alone. Now she agonized alone.

"And if we refuse?" asked Perseus, unintimidated by a voice from a stone head.

"Proud child, you are the cause of much of this. She must be delivered to the Kraken at the setting of the sun on the day indicated, or else the Kraken will be free to destroy Joppa and everyone within the city. For the insult that has been done to me, for the cruel injury you inflicted on my son, I demand the life of Andromeda."

"If I am the cause," Perseus replied firmly, approaching the stone head, "then I should make the restitution. Let the Kraken have me instead."

"It is too late. I have spoken. Andromeda is to be the sacrifice. In thirty days."

There was a rumbling and the headless statue split in two. Screams filled the temple and the priests bowed low in fear. His brave offer rebuffed, Perseus was once again the willing but perplexed youngster, uncertain what to do next.

As the people streamed out of the temple, the remnant of the once magnificent sculpture toppled forward, scattering queen, soldiers and priests. It shattered with a thunderous roar against the marble flooring, and with it, the dreams of the queen who'd ordered it raised.

No flute or lyre music filled Cassiopeia's private chambers that night. No dancer spun lithely above the mosaic tiles, no exotic dishes were proudly brought forth from the royal kitchens by the queen's chefs.

No entertainers plied their raucous trade in the taverns bordering the market stalls. Even the usually hysteric waterfront was quiet, the only movement coming from traders and merchants of other lands. They had learned quickly of the events which had taken place that afternoon in the temple and were anxious to finish their business well before another thirty days passed in Joppa. When that period ended, harbor as well as city would be deserted.

The mood in the royal chamber was even more somber than that afflicting the city at large. Though the cause was immortal and beyond human reach, and the danger older than recorded time, the assembly sitting in that chamber still had the air of a council of war.

Perseus and Ammon attended. They were joined by five of the most experienced and respected officers of the queen's household guard. Old Thallo was one of them. His four comrades differed in size and attitude, but they represented the best military minds of Joppa.

Loyalty and experience would not be enough this time, however. They needed a miracle, and miracles were not to be bought in the city's subdued marketplace.

One brilliant tactician was absent from that council, however. Queen Cassiopeia had fainted in the temple. Now she lay feverish and moaning in her bedchamber, begging forgiveness from a goddess who would not listen, more vulnerable in her delirium than ever she'd been on the throne.

But Andromeda was present. It was not her proper place to attend such a council, but it was her fate that would be decided there. If it was the will of the majority that she perish on the rocks beyond the harbor, she wanted to learn of it firsthand. So she stood quietly in the shadows and listened to the men.

Perseus could not sit still. He had already paced the floor for an hour, wishing for the unthinkable: an immortal throat under his fingers. In an hour he'd wasted more energy than most men use in a week.

"Is there any chance the goddess might relent and forgive Cassiopeia?"

"I think not, my boy." Ammon would not be falsely encouraging, for all that it troubled him to see the youth so tormented.

"She has announced her demand. To withdraw it would be to admit she was wrong in pronouncing it in the first place. Gods and goddesses must give the impression they are always right. If they were to change their minds like ordinary mortals, men might start to question them and begin to ignore their decisions."

"What about this Kraken, then? There must be some way to kill it."

Ammon laughed, not condescendingly. "My boy, I'm damned if I don't think you'd give it a try. But when the blood runs hot, memory runs short. You forget what happened to Argos."

Nervous words were passed between the soldiers.

"The Kraken is the last of the Titans," Ammon continued, "the last of those great immortal beings who fought alongside Cronos against Zeus. It would take a god to kill it, and they say only Poseidon and Zeus among all the gods can control it. As for killing it, there is no way it can be done—no way known to man."

"And you claim to be an optimist," Perseus said bitterly.

"So I am, yes. I believe strongly in the ability of man to eventually overcome most obstacles. But I am also a realist, young Perseus." He shook a cautioning finger at the frustrated youth.

"I believe in struggle, but not in needless sacrifice. If the entire city of Argos could not halt the actions of the Kraken, much less injure it, what can we hope to do?" He shook his head sadly. "Why must men become involved with the gods, when men are capable of confusing things sufficiently all by themselves?"

"Old friend, I've had just about enough of your philosophy. Words will not save Andromeda. If there is nothing else proposed, I will try to disable this monster by myself."

A soldier named Menas grinned ruefully at him. "Brave stranger, would you stab it in a toe? And you will have to swim to join battle with it, for the tale says much of Argos was destroyed by huge waves rised by the Kraken before it ever came close to the city."

"I'm a strong swimmer."

"And a brave fighter," Ammon agreed, "but bravery will not be enough to dissuade the Kraken. It has wrestled with Zeus. Would you do that too?"

"I would do anything if I thought I had a chance of saving Andromeda," he shot back. "Hades, but we must do *something*! I will not surrender the princess to appease the injured pride of a fickle goddess!"

A silence greeted his words, that voiced the feelings of his companions more clearly than any response could have.

Finally the officer called Solon spoke up. "Prince Perseus, we all love the Princess Andromeda and would give our own lives to save her. You must know that. We are pledged to it."

Murmurs of agreement rose from his fellow warriors.

"But what is the use of dying if only death is served?"

"We must have some reasonable chance of success before it is worth taking that risk," put in Castor.

"One moment, please, gentlemen." Everyone turned to face Ammon, who had been content until now simply to watch while they talked out their fears.

"I said there was no way known to man to slay the Kraken," he said smiling. "There might be a way known to woman."

"How you love your riddles, old poet." Abruptly, Perseus's anger softened and he smiled back. "Well then, for those of us poor mortals not the master of words that you are, unravel your puzzle to us."

"There is more to it than you think, Perseus. I said there might be a way known to woman—woman thrice over. To be specific, three old, blind women gifted beyond all others of the Earth in the ways of prophecy. Three women as knowledgeable as they are ancient."

"Who are they?"

"The Stygian Witches, or so they have come to be called. They live well beyond the desert frontiers of Joppa, in the mountains of the north, toward Persia."

"Damn them, old fool, and you with

them." Everyone turned to stare in surprise at Thallo. The usually phlegmatic warrior had bounded to his feet and was glaring at Ammon.

"Even if you found them, even if they showed you a way to defeat the Kraken, you would not live to use their advice."

"Why not?" Perseus asked, staring at him.

"It is said, sir, that they have a finely honed craving for human flesh. Once when the plague infested the city, the queen sent ambassadors to consult the blind oracles."

"Aye, I remember that time, though I was a youngster then." Menas regarded his colleague thoughtfully.

"And do you remember what happened?"

"Indeed," replied the soldier feelingly. "The ambassadors never came back."

"Nevertheless," Ammon insisted, "they are the only ones who might know a way to divert the Kraken, if not to slay it." He chewed his lower lip. "But their shrine is many days journey from Joppa, and we have only thirty given to us."

"That is no problem," Perseus assured him. "To Pegasus three days will be no more than three hours."

"The stallion of the air! Bless my soul, my boy, I'd forgotten." He scratched tiredly at his thinning hair. "Getting old, when I can't keep all the elements of the plot together."

Perseus clapped him on the back. "Never mind, old friend. You have offered a chance, and I will take it. I'll return with the information we need as soon as possible." He started out with the others close behind.

A pleading voice from behind halted them: "Perseus, take me with you."

Andromeda stepped out into the light and walked toward them. "If only as far as the Wells of the Moon. Just so that I may be with you a while longer."

Perseus gazed at Ammon, then Thallo. The poet glanced away and the old soldier simply shrugged.

"I may be going to my death," he told her softly.

Her reaction was not what he expected: she laughed. "I would rather die at the hands of a witch than in the jaws of the Kraken. If I am to be devoured, far better by something human than by some ancient monster."

"But the demand of the goddess," Solon hastened to remind her.

She looked sharply at him. "What should it matter to her how I die? She will have gained my death and that is what she wishes. And perhaps Perseus's as well. We may die together. That should please her." Her eyes turned back to stare into Perseus's own.

He held out a hand. She slipped hers into it.

It is known that when the gods are angry, the storms roiling atop Olympus are more violent than anywhere else in the world. Less is certain about the weather when the immortal inhabitants of that mountaintop dimension are merely irritated and confused.

Thetis stood before the throne of Zeus. Behind her stood Poseidon, Hera, Aphrodite and Athene, with the owl who served her as the symbol of wisdom and learning. The owl had turned its back on the king of the gods as though signifying its own disapproval of the course events were taking down on Earth. But Zeus failed to notice the movement, for the owl was as sly as it was wise.

"Your judgment was harsh," the king of the gods muttered from atop his throne.

"By insulting me, they blasphemed against all the gods!" Thetis snapped at him. "Did anyone in that vast assembly in the temple of Joppa object to their queen's odious comparison? Did *anyone*? No!"

"There was an old priest who—" Athene started to whisper, but she broke off at a warning look from Hera. Things were complicated enough.

"Against even you this blasphemy strikes," the furious Thetis concluded.

"Yes, yes," Zeus agreed irritably, acknowledging Thetis's claim with a wave of one hand. "Then of course your decision must stand. Now leave me."

Thetis departed, looking satisfied and smug. Poseidon sighed, the sound of deep ocean currents, and trailed after her. No matter how hard he tried to stay clear of the arguments and quarrels of Olympus, it seemed he was always drawn in.

Of course, if Thetis was right . . . and Zeus *had* agreed with her. The sea god emphatically wished his brother had never consigned the Titan to his care.

Zeus stepped down from the throne and crossed to confront the three remaining goddesses. His hands were clasped behind his back and his manner was changing from despairing to determined. Hera watched him warily, all too familiar with that look. Her husband was plotting something.

"It seems that young Perseus is moving into danger."

"He will find the Kraken a somewhat more formidable foe than that reprehensible Calibos," Hera said, and her tone reflected that she was not entirely displeased with the path events were taking.

"And your helmet is lost to him now?" he asked Athene.

"Swallowed by the swamps, Father. Lost forever to man. A great pity, too; I took pride in its fashioning. It was a fine bit of work, to make the metal bend the light around it like that."

"I agree. A great pity—replace it with another gift."

"That's not fair," Hera objected. "Athene has already given her gift to the young man, as did Aphrodite and myself."

"It was agreed that he should have the assistance of all three of you until this matter was completely resolved. Thetis's intervention has postponed that resolution. Therefore, he is properly entitled to continuing aid from all of you. He retains the sword and shield." He looked sternly at Athene, for all that she was his favorite.

"Replace the gift."

"Another helmet?"

"No." For a moment he was silent, thinking.

"Perseus needs knowledge far more than weapons of war. This Ammon he has struck up a friendship with is an admirable and wily old mortal, but his wisdom is lacking in certain areas. That is what Perseus most requires. And you, daughter, goddess of wisdom, are best suited to see that he receives it."

"I cannot wave my hand and make him wise," she pointed out.

"No, but we can offer him proper council," he said, looking toward her shoulder. "Give him the wise companion, Bubo the owl. It can supply advice when advice is required. Give Perseus also the ability to understand the owl's talk. This is my wish. *And* my command."

At that, he turned and stalked away from them, much pleased with his decision.

"Never!" Mildest and most even-tempered of the goddesses, Athene was furious. "Father goes too far in his defense of this Perseus."

"It is Zeus's command." Hera was sympathetic. "You cannot disobey."

"No, I cannot." Her anger was quickly overtaken by busy thoughts. "I must give Perseus 'the wise companion, Bubo the owl.' So Father Zeus demands. An owl of mine named Bubo." She turned and walked off, muttering to herself.

"Now what do you suppose she's up to?" Aphrodite wondered aloud.

Hera watched the younger goddess disappear into the mists. "I don't know, mistress of affection." Then she grinned. "But if I know Athene, she will surprise us all, including Father Zeus."

The pool of water rested mirror-bright and unchanged near the center of the Wells of the Moon. Only Artemis's chariot had moved since the fateful night when man and horse had reached an understanding on this spot. It had turned slightly, and so the moon was no longer full.

The beat of wings sounded above the mating groans of frogs and the drone of night bugs. Pegasus dropped from the sky and landed on a slight rise overlooking the pond.

The stallion surveyed its territory. There was no sign of the man-friend it had come to love and serve. In heart and mind the horse knew he would soon return, and they would again skip clouds together.

Thirst impelled it down the gentle slope toward the water, where it bent and sipped noisily, sending spreading ripples across the still pond. There was a rustling from the far side of the surface but the horse did not hear it.

A crack split the night air and Pegasus's head jerked sharply upward. It was not the crack of thunder but a higher, unnatural sound. Something stung the stallion's neck and tightened around it.

Calibos dug his hoof into the earth and leaned back on the whip. He had it wrapped around the arm with his one hand and was shouting furious commands as the stallion bucked and reared.

The vegetation surrounding the pool erupted things that might once have been men. They swarmed around the kicking, neighing horse, carrying ropes and netting.

"Net!" Calibos roared. "Quickly, before it rises from the earth!"

Pegasus struggled violently, but the whip around its neck burned when it tried to pull free and Calibos's weight kept the stallion from positioning itself properly in order to fly.

The air was filled with nets. They were designed to catch creatures of the sea, but Calibos had suspected they would work with equal efficiency on something that swam through air.

The stallion continued to kick and to beat its mighty wings, but the harder it fought the more entangled it became in the nets. Entwined in the netting, its forelegs crossed. Finally it went down, bruising leg and wing alike.

Calibos felt confident enough now to let go of the whip. There was a burn the length of his forearm where the hide had rubbed off the skin, but he felt only pleasure as he limped toward his servants.

Additional nets were cast over the struggling, muscular prisoner until finally the great beast was exhausted. He lay on the damp earth, breathing heavily and eyeing Calibos with helpless fury.

The Lord of the Marsh stopped and bent close to the entangled head. "Well, intruder. No longer will you carry spies and troublemakers to my home. I toyed with your cousins. Their hunting once gave me pleasure and food. For that and for other things Zeus did this to me." He ran the fingers of his remaining hand across his misshapen features.

"But I could never quite trap *you*. You were always a little more clever, a little stronger than the others. But by taming you, that meddler Perseus caused you to relax your watchfulness just a trifle. Just enough.

"Let him do what he will now, but he will do it alone and not on the back of the master of the skies."

One sharp hoof kicked out suddenly. Calibos jumped back, but not in time. It caught him a glancing blow on one shin and he hobbled about in pain. There were unearthly giggles from the assembled swamp things. A stare from Calibos reduced them instantly to silence.

Gingerly feeling the bruise on his leg, the Lord of the Marsh glared at the stallion.

"A last defiance, my friend. I welcome the pain. It reminds me of the damage you have helped do to me, you and this Perseus. The pain is good. It will keep me from forgetting." He whirled, angrily addressed his servants.

"Make ready while I call the others with the cart. I do not fear Perseus and his friends, but the sooner we return home the longer I will have to relish this moment."

He pulled a crooked hunting horn from his belt. Its curved sides were covered with obscene cameos. A sharp, atonal bellow drifted across the Wells of the Moon, beckoning forth additional undead to give assistance to their lord.

The sounds ringing through a little-visited section of the Olympian domain were no less discordant, but they were sharp and metallic in contrast to the mournful baying of Calibos's horn.

This was a darker, dingier, less perfect region of the realm of the gods. Its master preferred it that way. Dirt could be found here, a discomfiting reminder of mortality. There was neither marble nor graceful columns. The air was heavy with soot and grime, not because the master of this place was unable to banish it, but because he found it comfortable.

In many ways Hephaestus was impatient with his godliness. Like the dour Poseidon, he had little use for the grandeur of Zeus's court or the intrigues that were hatched there. His concerns were somewhat less than cosmic. He preferred eternity uncomplicated.

Furthermore, he was lame, and knew his imperfection was a distasteful sight to his fellow gods and goddesses. It reminded them that for all their powers and immortality, they were less than perfect. Hephaestus did not even care much for nectar and ambrosia, oftentimes preferring more earthly, mundane nourishments.

Of all the gods, he was the most human.

At the moment he was seated working at his favorite workbench. A perpetual fire blazed behind him, his foundry kept hot by the diverted beating of Olympus's own volcanic heart. Strange metals had been forged in that blaze, alloys that would not be known to men for thousands of years.

At the moment, however, the god of the forge was playing with more common metals. Athene sat watching him from nearby, ignoring the soot that was accumulating on her immaculate gown. From her shoulder, the wisest of owls, snowy Bubo, looked on with huge, interested eyes.

At one end of the bench was a drawing of suprahuman complexity. Metal gears and wheels lay scattered across the workbench, filling buckets and barrels nearby, spilling onto the floor.

In front of Hephaestus and to one side, lay a peculiar ellipsoidal body. Next to it sat a strigiformian skull. It seemed impossible that such minute mechanical components could be fashioned in so crude-looking a forge, but while the fingers of the smith were thick and gross, they functioned with godlike delicacy and skills.

The lame god hunched over his table filing and shaping a few last pieces of his latest project. When Athene had first proposed the idea to him, he'd been reluctant to take it on, being busy with a backlog of thunderbolts for the ever-demanding Zeus.

But he was intrigued by the challenge she had given him. The idea of thwarting Father Zeus's command without disobeying it was too tempting for the slightly mischievous Hephaestus to decline.

So he'd collaborated on the plans with Athene, taking pleasure in her company, and had worked with all his skill and speed to finish the task before anyone else might learn of the intended deception.

Soon they would learn how successful his work had been. As to the likeness of the subject he had no doubts. He was justly proud of his skill—the little mechanical owl would be a perfect metal reproduction of the ancient bird now perched on Athene's shoulder.

The goddess of wisdom turned away from

the smith. She stroked the chest of the owl on her shoulder, running her fingers affectionately through the soft feathers.

"Hephaestus will do all he can, Bubo. Bronze and iron and strange new metals are no substitute for feathers, but he is very skilled and ingenious." Hephaestus looked up from his work momentarily and smiled at her, pleased by the compliment.

"Let great Zeus rage and thunder until even Olympus shakes, but I will never part with you, my beloved companion. And there is naught he can do, for I shall in truth be sending my 'wise companion, the owl Bubo' to the aid of Perseus, to give him advice and counsel. Only it shall not be the Bubo Father Zeus expects."

Content, the bird shifted slightly on her shoulder and issued a soft hoot of agreement.

IX

A less impressive owl mimicked the call of its immortal cousin on far distant Olympus with a querulous hooting. It was immediately drowned out by the blare of a trumpet.

A cluster of distraught and tired searchers met by the shore of a small lake. The moon watched them gather and said nothing. Artemis saw everything that happened during the night. Perceptive as that silent goddess was, however, and for all that she might be sympathetic to the poor humans who blundered about in the dark of her shadow, her lips would open wide only at a command from Father Zeus, who sometimes spoke to her from the vicinity of the constellation Ursa Major.

But this night the bear was quiet and still, and she would have to look on silently, without voicing her anxious feelings.

Philo dug at a thorn which had gotten stuck in his sandal. His companions gathered around him, their mounts puffing easily in the warm night air. Soon Perseus, Ammon, Andromeda, and the trumpeter were assembled alongside the water.

"We've searched the whole shoreline," Thallo told the others, patting the neck of his horse, "as well as several other ponds."

"No sign?"

"Nothing." Thallo turned and gestured back toward the water. "A few hoofprints down by the water's edge, but no tracks to follow."

"Of course not, you thick-witted swordsman," said a discouraged Ammon. "A horse that flies leaves no tracks to follow, unless one be a god, and we are not gods."

"You won't be a man much longer either, old mushmouth, if you don't watch your words." Thallo instinctively fingered the hilt of his sword.

"No quarreling here, among friends." Perseus urged his horse between them and favored each with a reproving glare. "We have no time for that, and even less now than we'd thought.

"We cannot wait here for Pegasus, whatever may have drawn him away. I'll set out to seek the Stygian Witches on my own, on a normal, earthbound horse."

"No," said Andromeda with conviction. "We will ride with you at least as far as the shrine which is supposed to be their home. It is a long and perilous journey and one man, however bold, stands little chance of success. There is too much at stake here to risk failure because of a sprained ankle or broken bone, Perseus, or because your mount might come up lame. A larger expedition will better serve us all."

"I agree that the journey is perilous," he told her. "Too perilous for a princess."

"I will be the judge of that." She smiled at him. "You are not yet my lord and master. Not yet! In the absence of the queen, it is I who command the household guard." She turned to the soldier holding the trumpet. "Herald!"

"Majesty?"

"Return to the city. Inform the queen of our failure to find the flying horse and that in consequence all of us will travel as escort for Prince Perseus."

The trumpeter backed his horse by way of salute, then turned and galloped for the city.

"His path is well marked. As for the rest of us,"—she gestured skyward—"we follow the north star. Hup!" She dug her heels into the flanks of her mount and rushed off northward, leaving a speechless Perseus waiting behind her.

His wits returned slowly. "Andromeda, no!" He whirled on Thallo. "Stop her!"

The officer struggled to keep a straight face, saying solemnly, "I am an officer of the royal household guards. I can take orders only from the queen, the princess, and my superior officers."

Perseus turned to his advisor. "Ammon!"

"Only one thing I can suggest, my boy. After all, she talked you into letting her come this far. Clever little dear, isn't she? Best follow her, before she gets too far ahead." And he whipped his own horse to a gallop, followed rapidly by Thallo and the other soldiers, and eventually by a bewildered Perseus.

Headstrong and foolish, he thought as he raced up alongside her. Yet I can only admire and love her for it. He watched as the princess, her gaze turned resolutely forward, appeared to flow over the landscape. She became one with her horse, and in the moonlight her veils trailed behind her like white flame.

I'm sorry for all this, Andromeda. I'm sorry Pegasus did not appear at the Wells of the Moon. I'm sorry for the danger that I've brought to you and your people. I'm sorry I've so confused your life.

She looked across at him and smiled behind her veil, and his last thought before setting his mind on the long ride to come was, Ah, but I'm not sorry I fell in love with you.

The moon watched the seven riders depart. So did the owls and the insects, the newts and frogs and toads.

One who was now a close cousin to the last of these slowly emerged from behind a thick tangle of roots. His tail swishing with nervous energy, he thoughtfully watched the little caravan start on its way. For the first time in a long while, Calibos was reasonably content with life.

The riders pressed their horses as hard as they drove themselves. Day by day the land grew progressively more barren. First the larger trees shrank and eventually vanished, the pines and the famed cedars. They conceded the land to brush and scattered palms. Soon even the bushes gave up the struggle for life and the last grasses faded into burnt brown shreds, or clung precariously to rain-holding crevices in the rocks.

In place of trees, the riders sought shade under the bare stone which thrust skyward in mockery of greener life. Water secreted itself in hard-to-find pools, and each morning the sun made itself known with increasing strength.

Phoenicia was a thin strip of life that backed onto a region fast changing from marginal farmland to naked desert. The core of long-dead trees hinted at what the land had once supported, and offered a warning about what could happen elsewhere if men of richer lands were careless with their soil.

Perseus wiped the sweat from his brow and galloped on ahead of his companions. The movements of his horse were listless and he increased his speed without enthusiasm. Here animals suffered as deeply as men.

Topping the little rise he'd espied, Perseus stared at the empty landscape revealed on the other side. Its colors were raw, its topography hellish: a dry hell that reminded the rider of almonds he'd seen spread out on blankets to dry in the sun. Everything here was like that:

brown and yellow. Nowhere could he see a place where even a witch might survive.

The others rode up alongside.

"What do you see, my boy?" Ammon shaded his eyes, squinting hard at the harsh terrain. "Curse these old eyes. I see nothing."

"Then you still see clearly, old friend. There *is* nothing. Nothing but more wilderness."

"No sign of the shrine?"

Perseus allowed himself a dry, tired laugh. "Shrine indeed! A shrine to the dead, maybe. This land is unfit even for eaters of carrion." He gestured toward the distant, wavering horizon.

"Everywhere you look it is the same. We could be lost forever in such desolation."

Andromeda nudged her horse. She'd been gazing not at the forbidding land ahead, but at the startlingly blue sky. Something above held her attention. She studied it just long enough to make certain it wasn't something her brain had conjured out of the heat.

"Look. Up toward those far cliffs."

Perseus and the others turned. One by one, they too noticed the object which had caught the princess's attention.

Now it was in line just above and to the right of a tall dead tree—a sudden, winking streak of light against the otherwise uninterrupted blueness.

The horses offered their own form of confirmation. They were waking from the stupor engendered by the midday heat. Their now alert eyes lifted and they began to shift nervously in place.

Perseus dismounted and worked to calm his own mount. So did Thallo, who suddenly pointed to his left. "There! There it is again."

"It's flying straight for us."

"Perhaps Pegasus has managed to follow us, sir," suggested the ever-hopeful Solon.

"I think not." Perseus squinted into the light, but could not identify the approaching mystery. "The stallion was never so bright, not even on a cloudless day such as this. No, it's something else."

"One of Calibos's evil creatures?" Thallo suggested, and instantly regretted the remark because of the expression it brought forth from the princess.

"Well, it won't find us cowering under the rocks." Philo dismounted quickly, as did the other soldiers. Swords were drawn and readied.

"Whatever it is, it can't be very big." Thallo shielded his eyes. "A hawk?"

As the apparition was moving quite near now, no one responded to Thallo. The thing was generating a most peculiar sound, like wingbeats, but oddly stiff. There was also a slight hum from it, a cross between a whirr and a rattling, that none could identify.

"No hawk I ever saw," said Ammon tensely. "Do you think it's going to attack?" He took a step closer to his horse, who continued to stir uneasily as the object approached. Nearing the dead tree, it began to slow, and as the sunlight faded from its surface, its outline grew visible. The eyes of the watchers widened as they identified the shape, but everyone was too fascinated to speak. They simply stood and stared, their weapons held loose and half-forgotten at their sides.

As it closed on the tree, the shining owl-shape began to brake sharply. That it was an owl could not be doubted, but it was unlike any other owl that had ever been.

In place of feathers it boasted rectangular metal plates, overlapping and highly polished. Tubular legs ended in metal talons, and the great rounded eyes flashed and spun with energy derived from a nonbiologic source. They gleamed bright red, like tiny windows in the night.

It clanked perceptibly as it approached the tree and let out a loud "Hoo! Hoo!" of warning. The sound was cousin to a normal owl call, but throatier and decidedly metallic. It spooked the horses, and Thallo and his friends were hard put to control them.

"By all the gods!" Ammon finally muttered, breaking the mesmerized silence. "That I should live to witness such a wonder!"

"An owl. A golden owl of metal that lives." Perseus started toward the tree, his initial fearfulness overcome by his curiosity.

The manifestation hovered, lowered its talons, and carefully gripped a branch. For a moment it swayed precariously on its newly won perch, then held steady. It let out a brazen hoot of triumph, at which point the rotten wood cracked, dropping the unprepared bird onto the sandy soil below. It lay there, clicking and whirring peevishly.

Perseus was the first to reach it. He bent, ignoring those sharp metal talons, and set the creature upright. Bright red eyes turned on him and the owl clicked away merrily, its attention now wholly on its rescuer.

The others slowed. Only Ammon and Andromeda moved to stand next to Perseus. The soldiers remained slightly behind, superstition temporarily reining in their natural curiosity. They watched warily as Perseus and the princess studied the creature, and in the manner of soldiers offered silent invocations to their personal deities.

"Too heavy for that old, dead branch," Perseus explained to his companions as he examined the broken tree limb.

Ammon's gaze narrowed as he stared at the youth. "Now, how do you know that?"

"He told me so."

"Told you?" Andromeda's gaze shifted from her betrothed back down to the bird.

It continued to wheeze away enthusiastically, clicking and whistling gleefully.

Perseus nodded. "He says his name is Bubo."

"You got that name out of all those clicks and buzzes?" Ammon looked doubtful.

"What clicks and buzzes?" Perseus

frowned, looking puzzled. "His speech is perfectly clear to me."

"And what is perfectly clear to me," Ammon replied with assurance, "is that this magical creature is another gift to you from the gods, like the sword and helmet and the shield." He sounded relieved as he spoke to the other attentive members of the parched group.

"This does not by any means insure the success of our expedition, but to know that at least someone among the immortals favors our young friend here must be regarded as an encouraging sign."

"Perhaps," said Solon, not so ready to concede the old poet's point. "But we know for a fact that we are opposed by the goddess Thetis."

"We are far from the ocean here," argued Philo, "and far from her reach."

Menas made a sign and gazed skyward. "One is never far from the reach of the gods."

"Nevertheless, you must all agree that this is a good sign." Ammon stroked his beard and looked speculatively at the owl. "The question before us now is, can it possibly be more than just a sign?"

"It is." Perseus watched fondly as the creature hopped up and down experimentally. Its head turned a complete circle and the red eyes came to rest on him. "As you have surmised, it is here to help us, good Ammon."

Thallo sounded doubtful. "A thing of metal and wheels—a child's toy. What can it possibly do for us?"

This produced a distinctly irritated sputter from the object of their discussion.

"For a start," Perseus translated for them, "he says he can lead us to the shrine."

The suspicious old soldier nodded approvingly. "If it can do that, then it is indeed more than a child's toy."

An outraged whistle came from the owl. It hummed with more patience at Perseus. Obediently the youth picked it up, staring in wonder as it spread metal wings. They creaked slightly.

Then the wings became a blur, there was a louder humming, and the marvelous manifestation shot skyward with a speed no flier of flesh and bone could have matched.

At a modest altitude the owl leveled off and commenced flying northeastward. It returned, circled above them, and repeated the pattern.

Perseus nudged his rested horse. They left the dead tree behind, carefully tracking the owl's path. From time to time it would pause and circle overhead to make sure the animate dots on the hot earth below were still following.

They crossed over the rise and down into the desolate valley, but did not continue straight across the barren plain. After an hour's journey they were directed to turn sharply to their left. The new path led down a narrow wadi. Towering walls of gray and yellow stone rose high above them. The sides of the little canyon soon grew so narrow that the horsemen had to make their way forward in single file.

Occasionally one of the horses would start and utter an uneasy whinny, yet anxious glances to left and right always found only bare stone blotched by an isolated clump of desert scrub.

A warm fog began to rise about them, issuing from cracks in the rock. Perseus placed his hand close to one such opening, only to draw it back hurriedly.

"This rock is on fire!"

"Not on fire, my boy," Ammon explained patiently. "The heat emerges from below. I have observed such places before, most notably by the famous royal mineral baths at Thebes."

"I didn't know you'd traveled in Aegypt, sir," said Perseus respectfully.

Ammon chuckled. "I've visited many lands, my boy. I finally settled in Joppa because the climate suited me, both in body and in mind. Half of that still applies, and perhaps soon we will be able to help fix the half that's gone sour."

"Where does the heat come from?" asked the interested Andromeda. "Hades?"

He shrugged. "No one knows, my dear. Some would say Hades, yes. Others think elsewhere. I do not pretend to know. I am a poet, not a natural philosopher."

The mist caressed them, writhing about

the mounts and their riders; there was an air of mischievous, inimical intelligence about it.

They soon left it behind. Occasionally Perseus would look upward, to see a bright star moving in the sky. It kept just ahead of them, pausing and circling from time to time to let them catch up before continuing on its course. He thought he could hear a reassuring hoot from it.

The wadi bent and came to an end which opened onto another, smaller valley ending in a sheer escarpment. Pine trees crowning that far cliff looked short as grass.

They stopped at the end of the canyon. Across the valley and atop the cliff were the ruins of an ancient temple.

Once it had dominated the cliffs and all the land around it. A vicious prince had ruled from that impregnable fortress, extorting tribute from all who came through his territory. Now the prince and his bandits were less than memory, their wealth availing them nothing.

The valley was soon crossed. Bubo was waiting for them, perched on a sharp spear of stone, a perch less likely to crumble rudely beneath him. The riders dismounted and surveyed their intended destination.

Instead of being discouraged by the dangerous climb ahead, Perseus was overjoyed. The shrine was real, a fact he'd doubted in private. Whether its mysterious, rumored inhabitants actually existed was still a matter for conjecture.

But the shrine, at least, was real.

He embraced Andromeda and then joined his companions in preparing for the ascent. The shield of Hera was strapped securely to his back. From his belt hung the sword of Aphrodite.

"You and Ammon can wait here for us," he told the princess.

"I'm coming with—"

"No, illuminator of eternal love. I think not this time."

"I still command the soldiers of Joppa," she reminded him.

"Then command them wisely, so that they may help and not hinder me. You ride like a dragonfly, my life, but you have not the muscles or experience for a climb such as this. It is best we all look clearly and reasoningly at our individual limits, or disaster will befall us for certain."

He turned and gestured upward. "Tell me truthfully that you believe you can make this climb, and I shall object no more."

She studied the cliff face, the soft sandstone, the narrow ledges, the places where a climber would have to pull himself bodily to the next level by sheer strength. Then she grimaced and looked away.

"I can't. You are right, husband-to-be. I will stay behind."

"Someone has to stay and guard the

horses," Ammon told her sympathetically. "That could be as vital to our success as anything else. And poor old man that I am, I could not do it alone." He winked surreptitiously at Perseus.

"Then I will remain," she said firmly to Perseus, "and await your return. Go quickly now, before I forget myself." She kissed him hungrily. The soldiers half turned aside and whispered amusedly.

"I will be quick," he assured her with a warm smile as they separated, "but though you may forget yourself, know that I never could." He turned and started lithely up the rocks.

The two below watched the party ascend. After a while Andromeda casually remarked to her elderly companion, "You have been giving my love lessons in the wiles of a lover's speech."

Ammon shook his head. "Nay, my lady." He squinted as he tried to keep the climbers in focus. "He has not yet the skills of a poet, your Perseus. But he has the heart of one. His words to you come from there, not from any lessons of mine."

They lapsed into silence as they watched the climbers shrink from view.

The climb was no less difficult than the men had expected. The sun hammered the face of the cliff relentlessly, driving strength and water from their bodies.

Fortunately, whenever exhaustion threatened to become total, a wide ledge would suddenly appear, or a cave cut by wind and water into the soft stone, and there they would rest and gather their strength.

Then they would resume the ascent. Near the top the escarpment rounded off somewhat and the going became easier. Unexpectedly, a newly gained ledge turned out to be the crest, and they found themselves standing on the edge of the summit, the rubble of the once-magnificent temple facing them.

Menas peered cautiously inward, sniffed and turned away gagging. "Prince Perseus, I would rather suffer the odor of the slaughter-house than that which comes from within."

"I think your appraisal not as far off as you might think, Menas. It has the stink of the charnel house all about it. Can you see anything?"

"Nothing."

They moved nearer. Perseus pointed. "There. A light of some kind."

"A fire," suggested Castor.

They entered the ruins, Thallo cautioning all to keep swords and wits at the ready and each man to be aware of his neighbor.

The remnants of the temple were devoid of the magnificence that had once ruled here. The building itself was all that remained. Though cloaked in grease and soot, the columns were unbroken, a tribute to the slave workers who'd raised them. But most of the interior wall was gone, and the faint light reflected not off marble or mosaic but bare rock.

The interior was home to a million rats. They swarmed in front of the stalking men and closed in curiously behind them. Their constant inquisitive chattering sounded like running water in old pipes. They watched the men out of anxious little red eyes. Though they smelled blood they did not try to bite. They knew better. Men could kill.

The time for feasting would come soon enough.

Philo stumbled over something, cursed and kicked it. It ricocheted hollowly off a far wall.

"Not a rock," muttered Thallo, in reaction to his comrade's curse. He pointed with his sword toward the object Philo had kicked. "A human skull."

Menas was bent over, examining the debris which littered the floor to a depth of half a foot in places. "Here's another," he informed them. "And there another. Plenty of other bones, too." He gingerly picked up a hand and forearm, ran a finger along a scored section of ulna. "Gnawed."

He hastily tossed it aside. He was a soldier and he'd seen bones before, but those times the cause of death had always been obvious. He looked over his shoulder toward the entrance. It seemed leagues distant.

The fire Perseus had spotted danced against the far wall. A crumbling mosaic depicting unwholesome rites reflected some of the glow back into the center of the temple chamber and provided enough light to see by. Crouched around the flames were three figures. They moved slowly.

Perseus and his companions came forward quietly through the darkness.

The three figures stirred a liquid which bubbled noisily inside an old cauldron. Their hair was long, stringy, and matted with dirt. Clothing no thicker than fog covered skin tough and wrinkled as papyrus. Perseus wondered if those gaunt frames contained any blood. Certainly their stock of humanity was low.

Despite the quiet approach of sandaled feet, the noise soon reached the three sisters. All sniffed at the air. One held a round crystal to her forehead and searched the darkness. The crystal looked very much like an eye.

"Someone coming."

"Sounds like a man," said another. "A young man. Who has the eye?" she asked eagerly.

"I do," announced the third.

"Give it to me."

"No." The witch manipulating the crystal orb moved away, clutching it protectively. "I want to be the first to see him."

"Is he really young?" asked the first witch, more patient than her companions. "Perhaps he's fine and plump. What do you see, sister? Tell us."

"Yes, what do you see?" The other left off

her stirring and turned an eyeless face toward the center of the chamber. Behind her the pot continued to bubble.

Perseus moved closer. He'd slipped the shield from his back and now wore it on his left arm. The sword hung ready from his right hand.

"Yes, yes," hissed the witch with the eye. "A young man. Not plump, but well made. Healthy also, by the look of him, and tall."

"Lots of meat on him, sister?" inquired the first witch. She licked her lips noisily. In the dark it sounded like a file working metal.

"Enough for all three of us, sister, if we're none of us too greedy."

"Who's greedy?" snorted the second witch. "Are you calling me greedy?"

"Hush now," the first witch ordered firmly, "lest we frighten our nice young visitor away. We wouldn't want that, would we, sisters?"

The three chuckled softly, waiting. From the corners of the chamber the rats watched expectantly.

Perseus halted well away from them and lifted his sword by way of greeting. "Have no fear, ladies. I come in peace."

"So much the better," said the third witch softly. "Tall you say? Fresh and tender?"

"Let me see him," demanded the first witch, having had enough of blind patience. She snatched the crystal eye from her sister's fingers and set it into her own forehead. A smile slid over her face. Perseus watched their movements with apparent unconcern.

"Ah, that's much better. Yes, a fine, healthy young man. Come a little closer, young visitor." Her voice was a plaintive, harmless whine.

"Yes," said the second, equally coaxing, "so that we may see you better." She took the eye from her sister.

"A fine young fellow," she whispered.

"We are honored by your visit," said the first witch in grandmotherly fashion. She let out a sigh. "We are so lonely here, so isolated. We are shunned by the ignorant, who will not even make use of our talents, and so we dwell in misery with no one else to talk to."

"What can we do to help you?" asked the third witch.

"What you might expect." Perseus had not lowered shield or sword, nor had he taken the first witch's suggestion and moved nearer. "I need your advice."

"You'll really have to come a little closer," the second witch implored him. "My sisters and I are a little deaf, you see. Especially Cycorax here, the youngest. Such a pity that she should go deaf so young—only three hundred and forty years old."

"Three hundred and thirty-eight," the third witch reminded her sharply.

Perseus took another couple of steps forward. "There," he asked loudly, "is that better now?"

The first witch shook her head. "I still can't hear him clearly, this fine young man."

"What if we moved a little closer to him?" suggested the second sister. "That would help."

"Yes, much easier, much simpler to talk to him that way," agreed the third.

They left their cauldron and its foul contents and moved down from the dais it rested upon, shuffling slowly and with mock difficulty onto the main floor. As they did so they wandered apart, as would only be natural for three sightless women. But somehow Perseus remained centered between them.

They did not think to search behind them, near the top of the mosaic pediment where Thallo and the other four officers waited with a silent metallic owl and watched quietly.

Perseus, beginning to have trouble keeping all three crones in sight, shouted, "Now!"

With an assist from Thallo the metal owl launched itself into the fetid air, screeching softly and clicking like a new clock as he climbed ceilingward.

The third witch frowned at the unusual noise but like her sisters was too overcome by the proximity of healthy young flesh to pay much attention to anything else.

Bubo banked sharply near the apex of the crumbling dome and dove downward.

"The eye," Perseus yelled as he waited for the attack, "Bubo, go for the eye!"

The original plan had called for Perseus and the owl to occupy the witches so his companions could surprise them from behind, but the owl's aerial abilities had sparked a fresh idea in the youth's mind.

Red eyes spun like a magician's pendant as the owl altered its approach in response to Perseus's order. He swooped in low and fast over the second witch. She reacted an instant too late. Her inhuman strength, which had enabled her and her sisters to overcome stronger warriors than Perseus and his companions, did not include unusual agility.

One metal talon dipped like a surgeon's knife at just the right instant and plucked the crystal orb from her hand. She snatched upward but the thief was already out of reach. A fight with Perseus was on her mind, not an attack from above.

Bubo let out a rattle of triumph as he soared low and let the eye drop. Holding his sword momentarily under his shield arm, Perseus caught the sparkling globe neatly.

Thallo and the others cheered as they scrambled down from the mosaic pediment. Bubo executed a little aerial jig and then resumed his perch on the rocks.

"The eye!" the second witch was screaming. "I've lost the eye!" She bent over and started scrabbling among the bones. "Foul trickery, sisters!" Her fury was directed at Perseus. "What have you done with the eye, stranger? Tell me, or you and your friends will become less than this!" and she lifted a rock the size of her fist and ground it to dust between her gnarled palms.

The display of strength caused Perseus to lift the eye high over his head. He stood studying it while the three evil sisters spent a few minutes contemplating a stew of a different sort than the one they'd anticipated.

Their fingers clawed frantically at the garbage carpeting the floor.

"We must have it, where is it?" babbled the second witch.

"Where?" echoed the third. "Tell us, or you will all surely die."

"You would have killed us anyway, witch," Perseus responded sharply, unimpressed by the threat.

"A rotten lie, stranger!"

"Rotten it is, but the truth. Rotten as this place and your souls. You don't frighten me with your threats, witch. Not now.

"As to the eye, never fear. It is safe . . . for the moment."

"Give it back to us now," screeched the first witch hysterically. "Give it back! Back! Back! We can't see anything without it."

"On one condition will I return it."

"Anything you ask," agreed the third witch.

"But we must have it now," added the first desperately.

"Your attitude shifts like a spring storm. No," he told them resolutely. "You'll have it back, I promise, but only after you've answered my question. I've come a long, hard way to ask it and I'm growing impatient. Hurry and decide, or an accident may befall your eye. Can you see with it if it's all in pieces?"

"Horrible, evil boy!" growled the second witch threateningly. "You would never do such a thing to three poor blind old women!"

"How many innocent travelers have you welcomed to the shelter of this place, only to slaughter them mercilessly? How many children have you devoured while their helpless parents watched and begged mercy of you, before you consumed them also?

"I know you for what you are, you three mothers of evil, so don't plead with me. Strike the bargain and have back your accursed eye, or refuse and dwell in darkness forever."

"No, no!" the first witch shouted quickly. For the first time she sounded genuinely frightened. "Ask your question then, boy, so that we may have back our sight."

"And hurry," the third witch said.

Perseus took a deep breath. "How might a mortal man face and defeat the Kraken?"

The three witches, who until now had been voluble to the point of confusion, were struck speechless.

X

"Impossible," declared the second witch, eventually breaking the silence.

"Young man of an unknown flavor," said the first witch slowly, "your question is brief and uncomplicated, and so must be our answer.

"The Kraken is invulnerable, immune to the weapons of man. You cannot fight the last of the Titans with spear and sword. His skin is like iron and his teeth can turn granite to hash. A thousand men could not bother him. He would sweep them aside with one arm and drown them in the sea."

"What about a catapult arrow fashioned from the log of a single great tree?" asked Thallo from the darkness.

"Hercules himself could heave such a

weapon, only to see it bounce off the Kraken's chest, bold soldier." The witch waved a warning finger toward the source of Thallo's voice.

"You could throw a mountain at the Titan and it would only be amused. You cannot drown it. It has no animal fear of fire; its skin would protect it were the whole world burning."

"An army could not kill it," the third witch added.

"You say it's impossible," Perseus said, keeping his attention on the witches' movements as he spoke. "Nothing is impossible. Nothing is invulnerable. Zeus and the other Olympians slew the rest of the Titans."

"You are no god, boy, fighting for control of the universe."

"There must be a way."

The third witch became suddenly thoughtful. "Perhaps one way."

The second faced her in confusion. "Sister, you have become senile as well as blind."

"Not I." She sniffed disdainfully and dismissed the remark. "You all talk of mortal men and mortal weapons. A mortal man may destroy with the assistance of immortal powers. That route is even more dangerous in its subtle fashion than the Kraken itself. The Kraken can be avoided. Once engaged, the way I have in mind can be instantly fatal."

"Tell me this way," Perseus urged her.

"Give me the eye and I'll tell you."

"Sly witch, do not think you can bargain with me. This is no marketplace. I will fight the Kraken with or without your advice."

"Then you will die," said the third witch coldly.

"And you three will live in blackness for eternity."

"Very well," she sighed. "It requires the head of Medusa, the Gorgon."

"Of course, of course!" exclaimed the first witch excitedly. "Yes, that might accomplish your end, boy. One look from the head of Medusa, be she dead or alive, will turn any living thing into stone, no matter how huge or powerful it may be."

"And her blood is a weapon as well. A deadly venom. She has two ways to kill," added the third witch.

"Yes, yes, the head of Medusa could overcome the Kraken," agreed the second.

"A Titan against a Gorgon," cackled the third witch. Her sisters joined in a coarse laughter which Perseus found utterly revolting.

"Ah, but first you must win Medusa's head, bold boy of the nasty caution," the first warned him.

"She's not going to give it to you," put in the second, laughing harder than ever.

"As a present!" the third concluded mockingly.

The first witch continued to admonish her intent listener, shaking a warning finger.

"Medusa's as difficult and dangerous in a fight as a dozen Krakens. Not as strong, it's true, but she has no need of strength. And she's far quicker. Are you quick of eye, boy?" More ghastly laughter from the other sisters. "You'll need more than quick wits to defeat Medusa."

"You'll not find her so easy to trick as we harmless old women," chuckled the second witch.

"It's your only chance if you mean to go against the Kraken," the third assured him. Then she frowned and asked, "Why do you intend to risk such a confrontation?"

"To save a city and the woman I love."

"Pfagh!" The second witch spat to one side, yellow phlegm spotting the floor. "How foolish you are, young man. There are many cities and many women you could conquer without having to battle a Titan."

"Don't waste your time, Sister," the third witch advised. "Mark that sweet-sour aroma that swirls about him. The boy's in love."

"Then not only does he lack the quick wits he'll need," observed the first witch, "he has no wits left at all!" Her cackle was brief and her tone turned serious again.

"Now give us back our eye, boy. We have answered your question."

"Yes, give it back." The third witch held out eager fingers ending in claws.

"I've not yet finished with my question. If, even after death, the face of Medusa can turn any onlooker to stone, what of her blood? Does it retain its potency?"

"Yes, yes. Deadly as when alive, until the last drop has dried."

"Then if I gain her head, how am I to handle it without getting the blood on me?"

"Poisonous and corrosive it stays," said the first witch, "and would burn through any container. No bottle or flask could restrain that blood. But you have touched the eye—*our* eye. Are you by chance wearing anything the color of blood, anything of red?"

"My cloak happens to be red."

"Good. That should do you ... *if* you get that far. Just as the eye has the power to give us sight, so the caress you give it will make your red cloak proof against the Gorgon's blood. I declare this so, by the powers of Hades and the eye. Wrap a portion of your cloak completely around the crystal and hold it still for a moment."

Perseus followed the instructions. A slight warmth seemed to emanate from the eye, heating his hands through the folds of material. It grew almost too hot to hold, then abruptly cooled to nothing.

"I've done as you instructed," he told them. "It grew hot."

"Has it cooled now?"

Perseus opened the folds and carefully touched the crystal. "Yes, completely."

"Then you have your shield, foolish boy. You must not touch the blood yourself.

"We can help you no more. Give us back our eye."

Perseus turned to his companions and gave a prearranged signal. Thallo nodded in acknowledgment. With Bubo clicking away overhead, the soldiers hurried around the circumference of the chamber and headed gratefully for the gap which opened onto clean air and daylight.

Perseus found himself alone with the three witches. "You have told me the truth?"

"We swear it," said the first witch.

"By all the gods of Olympus," added the third.

"By all the powers of Hades," the second finished.

"We have spoken only the truth," the first witch declared empathically. "We have done as you asked, have answered your question. The rest remains for you to do, for we cannot help you in that. Seek Medusa . . ."

". . . on the Isle of the Dead, where the River Styx broadens into a lake and touches the world of the living, at the very fringes of the Underworld," the third instructed him.

"And now the eye. As we speak the truth, you must keep your part of the bargain. You are bound to return the eye to us now, lest all the curses of the Fates befall you."

"And when I give it back to you," he said quietly, "what will happen then, when you have your sight back?"

"Ah," murmured the first witch through a

shrewd smile, "we will be able to see again. That's all."

"That's all?" Perseus nodding knowingly. "You will be able to see again? You'll also be able to see *me*, won't you? If I hand you the eye, will you not also try to take my hand with it?"

"Only in friendship," the first witch assured him demurely.

"Yes," added the second, "so that we might shake the hand of so worthy and clever an adversary."

"What else could we do?" asked the third. "Three poor old women?"

"You would take my hand, of that I'm certain. But not in friendship, I think. Most likely you'd take it all the way up to the shoulder, with the rest to follow later, over a hot, slow fire."

"You do us a great injustice, boy," said the first witch, her anger seeping through her grandmotherly manner. "In any case, you have agreed to the bargain we've struck. You must now give us back the eye." She held out eager claws.

"And so I will," Perseus said. "Here . . . catch!" And he tossed it toward them.

There was a tripartite shriek of rage and frustration. Stumbling into each other, the witches tried to catch the falling crystal. It fell between their weaving hands to land with a subdued clink among the bones and rotting leather and forgotten armor.

They bumped into one another, tripping in their haste to find their sight. Bones and skulls flew in all directions as they started digging through the garbage covering the floor. Perseus was forgotten.

"Where! Where is it?" they were shouting. "Where! I want it ... it's my turn ... give it to me!"

Still carefully staying out of reach, Perseus edged his way around the three harridans. Only when he'd finally succeeded in rejoining his companions outside the temple did he allow himself to relax.

Menas slapped him on the back, then looked distastefully back toward the noisome hole from which they'd emerged. "A foul place, Prince Perseus. I'd rather face a phalanx of Spartans than those three," he added, his expression emphasizing his words.

"We've gained what we came for," Perseus announced, breathing deeply of the fresh mountain air. "And also the enmity of the three Witches of Stygia. Let's begone from this place before they recover their eye. They might be able to see their way to some unknown revenge."

"I think not, sir." Thallo considered the temple opening thoughtfully. "Once they set to arguing, I'll venture it takes them a dozen years to settle things."

Everyone laughed, glad of the joke.

"Maybe so, good Thallo," Perseus agreed

with a smile, "but let's not stay here long enough to find out."

They started back down the mountain path, moving with care, the image of empty skulls and gnawed bones still fresh in their memories.

In that barren, forsaken country there was little that would burn. But like all soldiers, Thallo and his companions were no strangers to the ways of scavenging. Though tired from their ordeal in the temple and from the long, awkward descent down the cliff face, they still managed to locate enough brushwood and thornbush to fuel a comforting fire.

Now all were together again, well out of reach of any lingering animosity of the Stygian sisters. Their temple lay half a day's ride to the east. Nevertheless, Menas and the other officers were glad of the mountains that now lay between them and that abode of unwholesomeness.

The fire burned hot and fast before them. Castor and Solon lay against the warm rocks, chatting of the day's adventure and chewing the remnants of their supper. Thallo, Philos and Menas were curled up in their cloaks, already asleep and glad of it. Their comrades' conversation did not disturb them. Soldiers have the ability to sleep whenever the opportunity occurs.

Perseus and Andromeda had long since melted into each other's arms. Ammon dozed nearby. On a branch of a nearby tree—a live one, this time—the slightly tubby shape of Bubo the owl glowed rust red from the light of the flames his metal body reflected.

A soft neighing came from the horses. They were content despite the hard ride, having spent most of the morning at rest. Bubo joined them with a soft hoot, his metal owl eyes informing him that nothing stalked those seated or sleeping around the fire. Though no more than a tin doppelgänger, he took his assigned responsibilities seriously.

When not gazing into each other's eyes, Perseus and Andromeda stared solemnly into the fire. Each saw something different in the dancing flames.

Nearby, Ammon was not quite so content. He restlessly stirred the sand with a stick.

"The sands of time are running away like quicksilver, my young friends. Knowledge is useless without the time to employ it. Even Hercules did not have to rush from one labor to the next."

"You worry too much, old friend." Perseus smiled fondly at the tired playwright, whose beard shone silver by the fire.

"That's my way, boy. I suppose if I weren't such a worrier, I would never have become a writer. I'd have gone into a more respectable profession like goldsmithing or slave trading." He shrugged slightly. "But I do worry, and so I write."

"But you write comedies, good Ammon,"

Andromeda said and snuggled a little tighter against Perseus.

The poet grinned. "And the more I worry, the funnier my prose. I think that's the crux of comedy."

"This journey is no comedy." Perseus turned his gaze back to the fire. "According to Bubo, we'll be over these mountains sometime tomorrow." The owl hooted at the mention of his name.

"After that ... the Isle of the Dead."

"Which is no comedy for sure!" Andromeda said bleakly.

"And then Medusa." Ammon looked skyward, remembering. "I wrote a play about her long ago. Many writers have been inspired to do so." The stick played with the sand.

"In my youth I was partial to tragedy. That was before experience taught me that life was quite tragic enough without having to spend all my time writing about it! I don't like to spend my time brooding, and writers of tragedies invariably reflect what they're writing about. No thank you, I'll stick to comedies."

"Medusa ... forgive me, Ammon." Perseus looked embarrassed: "My formal education was somewhat neglected. She was a priestess of Aphrodite, I believe?"

"Not *too* neglected, my boy. You're right. She was a most beautiful woman, by all accounts. Beautiful enough to seduce a god, if she wanted to. She chose Poseidon.

"As it is told, they made love in the temple of Aphrodite, close by the altar itself, while Medusa laughed and joked and even taunted the goddess.

"It's said that Aphrodite is among the most tolerant and gentle of all the immortals, but this insult was too much even for her to forgive. So outraged was she that she transformed Medusa into a creature so hideous that one look from her would turn any living creature into stone." He grinned. "A perfect match for Calibos."

Andromeda looked earnestly at him. "Please. Even in jest, could we avoid mention of that name?" She shivered slightly, though the night was temperate.

Ah, you senile old fool, Ammon thought to himself. You have the manners and tact of a drunken elephant. That you who work with words should be so clumsy with them!

Andromeda had risen and walked away. Now Perseus hurried to join her, catching up with her just outside her tent.

"Ammon meant nothing, love. He was only trying to raise our spirits by distracting us from what lies ahead."

She turned, put her hands on his shoulders. "I know, he's a good person. It's just that anything that reminds me of Calibos..." She leaned against him and he held her close.

"Perseus, I'm so afraid for you."

"The Stygian Witches gave us no trouble."

"From what Thallo told me, you had time

and space to maneuver. If you make a single mistake with Medusa you'll have no chance to correct it, no chance at all. And she's not a feeble old woman."

"How do you know that? No one's seen her and returned to say what she looks like."

She looked uncertainly at him, then broke into a delighted, girlish smile. "You're teasing me," she said, but the smile faded. "I wish there were another way."

"I wish there were also," he confessed to her. "But there isn't, or the witches would have said so. They swore by Olympus and Hades that this was the only chance we have of dealing with the Kraken.

"Thetis cannot alter or withdraw her pronouncement. This thing must continue to its end, like a ball of string unraveling. There's nothing we mortals can do save try to make the string end where we choose." He gently pushed her away.

"My love, tomorrow you must return to Joppa with Ammon."

"No. We've already gone through this, Perseus. I'm coming with you. To the end of the world, if need be. Or in this case, to the beginning of the underworld."

He looked resigned. "Then sleep now. We'll all have a good rest and ride after the sun is up."

She entered the tent ahead of him. As she stretched out, he knelt to kiss her. She let her eyes close.

"So little time together, darling," she whispered. "So little time. . . ."

It was not difficult to ready the horses before daybreak. Supplies were silently packed and strapped on willing backs.

Ammon stood beside the dying, smoking fire and watched. Unperturbed at the prospect of being separated from their companions, the two untouched horses grazed peacefully nearby.

Perseus mounted his own steed, waved to Ammon. The poet nodded once and returned the salute. Joppa lay almost due south from their present position and he felt sure he could find the coast and a well-traveled road leading home. He was not especially sorry that Perseus had entrusted him with the princess's safe return. For all his voiced bravery he had no desire to visit the Isle of the Dead. His time to do that would come naturally and soon enough.

As for Medusa, one of Ammon's fondest dreams was that a bust of himself be placed in the theater outside Joppa; but he rather preferred it be fashioned by the normal arts of sculpture.

It seemed to Perseus as the morning wore on that he could hear the awakened princess sobbing, though he knew it had to be only his imagination.

He squinted at the sun. She would be awake by now, furious with Ammon for participating in the deception, distraught over the prospect of having to return to Joppa, and fearful for Perseus's safety.

First she would try to threaten and cajole Ammon into telling her the direction the riders had taken. Ammon would not tell her. Then she would search for hoofprints, but the riders had taken care to cover their departure well, and though resourceful, the princess was no tracker.

At last she would pack up camp with the poet and start on the long way back to Joppa; tearful, perhaps angry still, but on her way to safety. That was all that concerned Perseus. The Isle of the Dead was no place for a live young woman.

It was also no place for a live young man, he knew, but it helped his state of mind, knowing that she was out of danger.

"I'll come back, Andromeda, prepared to deal with the Kraken, or Thetis, or anyone else god or mortal who tries to force us apart!"

He'd made the pledge in a whisper, but Thallo had sharp ears. "An admirable vow, sir. Nothing finer to dedicate oneself to than love. Far better than a fickle people or callous king. That's why we ride with you now, instead of returning with the princess."

"It would be safer for you."

The old warrior took no offense. "A soldier can die only once, and this seems a cause worth dying for. And if we survive, what a tale we'll have to tell! Not to mention the gratitude of

Queen Cassiopeia. She'll double our pensions, at least."

But Perseus was not fooled by this mercenary appraisal.

Another two days brought them to a shoreline in a valley thick with fog. It was a fog that never rose, never dissipated, hanging just above the surface of the lake. Some said it was composed of the last breaths uttered by the living before they passed forever into the realm of the dead.

Unlike the abode of the Stygian Witches, however, this place produced no rotting miasma. The air was clean, crisp, and fresh with the ever-present fog. It was as sharp as death, that moist air. A casual traveler might breathe it and find nothing unusual to remark upon.

But it was special to the soldiers. They knew it well, having breathed of it on many occasions.

A small stream led them to the lake. It was flanked by tall reeds that shielded several dry rises. Perseus raised a hand as they neared a wide one and turned to Thallo.

"You understand your orders?"

The soldier nodded. "I'd prefer to go with you, sir, but I understand. Philo and I will wait for you until after dark. If you don't return—"

"If we don't return," Perseus finished for him, "it will mean that we've failed." His expression was unreadable. "Dead men travel in only one direction on the River Styx. At least if we fail we will not have far to travel to the land of the dead." He turned and studied the mournful fog.

"It's told in some tales that the river itself possesses strange powers. Time to see if any of the legends are true."

"Surely the Stygian Witches would not lie to us about Medusa's home," said Menas.

"Oh, *surely* not," Thallo said sarcastically, but he found himself half hoping the three evil sisters *had* lied; that Medusa did not await Perseus and the others somewhere in the center of this strangely peaceful lake.

But if they had, he reminded himself firmly, then there would be no hope for the Princess of Joppa. Nor for Perseus—and he'd come to like and admire the young prince. He'd make a fine, just ruler some day—the sort of ruler who'd respect the desires and take the advice of experienced old soldiers.

If Andromeda and Perseus perished, whether at the hand of the Kraken or otherwise, Joppa would be thrown into turmoil. Queen Cassiopeia was past childbearing age and Andromeda was her only heir.

With the succession shattered, there would be civil war the length and breadth of Phoenicia as pretenders and hopefuls vied for the crown. Joppa would suffer in the conflict, and Joppa was his home.

No, the witches had to have told the truth. They had to succeed here. Far more than a marriage was at stake. Had the vengeful Thetis foreseen the chaos that Andromeda's death would eventually create? If so, she was subtly having her revenge on the entire city while seeming to threaten only one member of its royal family.

Well, the gods might be immortal, but they're not all-seeing, he thought. Perseus had outwitted the Stygian Witches. There was a chance he might do the same with the Gorgon.

The riders had dismounted and unpacked their gear. Philo took charge of the mounts, led them to the nearby vegetation where they cropped contentedly at the lush foliage, unaware of the troubles vexing their masters.

Bubo sat on Thallo's pommel, ticking away smoothly. The little owl was far more than a simple device for providing advice and instruction, Thallo knew. Its presence was a sign that not all the gods wished the destruction of Perseus, Andromeda, and Joppa. He wished he'd been given Perseus's gift of making sense of its jumble of clicks, whistles, and hoots.

It was speaking to Perseus now. Thallo watched in wonder until the grim-faced prince rejoined them.

"Bubo says he cannot come with me. He is restrained from accompanying anyone to the Isle."

"Why?" asked Menas.

"He says that if he visits the Isle of the Dead his own life will stop. I do not completely understand, but apparently his life force is not as flexible as our own. That which drives him would stop if he were to go that close to the underworld. He will have to stay here and wait with you, Thallo. He can't go along."

From its resting place, the owl buzzed sadly.

"Well, I know something that does have to go along." He fumbled at his purse. "Here. You'll need this."

Perseus accepted the four silver coins, jingled them in his hand. "Thanks, my friend. Money's the last thing I thought we'd use on this quest."

"For Charon, the ferryman," Thallo explained. "If he'll carry you. You won't outwit him, but his price is well known. Unless you'd rather swim, that is."

"I've no desire to travel with him," was Perseus's reply, "but the River Styx is no place for a swimmer to lose his way, and we don't know in which direction the Isle of the Dead lies. We'll offer him his due, and hope our unusual 'state' doesn't put him off."

Turning, he started off through the reeds, accompanied by Castor, Menas, and Solon. Thallo and Philo watched them depart.

"May the gods go with them." Philo muttered sadly, securing the last of the horses to a dead stump selected for that purpose.

"Nay." Thallo shook his head and gazed unrepentingly skyward. The heavens remained dull gray. "Let the gods stay out of this. I'm of the same mind as that babbling old poet.

They've caused us enough trouble as it is. Why can't they be content with their own squabbles without always poking into the affairs of mortals?"

Philo looked nervous. "Hush, Thallo. One may overhear you."

"Let them hear me, then. Sooner or later we all travel down the River Styx, and soldiers sooner than most. What good's a man's life if he can't guide his own destiny?"

"Who says he can't?" Philo gestured toward the nearby lake. "Perseus is doing just that."

"A good point, my friend. Which is why I wish the gods would stay out of it. I have much confidence in Perseus. In the goodwill of the gods I have none."

It seemed more like the sea than a river to the four marchers when they eventually reached its shore. But the River of the Dead has no hard and fast dimensions. It can appear broad as an ocean one time, narrow as a creek the next. At the moment, it chose to look like an endless expanse of mist and water.

Save for that sense of endlessness and the perpetual fog that clung to it, there was nothing extraordinary about the place. The surface of the water was calm, peaceful. Yet despite the profusion of growth inland, no reed protruded above the surface. No water striders skated in its shallows, no frog called gruffly, no fish cracked the broad expanse of gray.

It was quite appropriately, Perseus thought as he surveyed the serene waterscape, dead calm.

To left and right high cliffs emerged from the shore. Somewhere ahead of them across the water rose the barren crags of the Isle of the Dead. Somewhere in the center of the lake river/state of mind.

A narrow beach of dark sand formed a line between shrubbery and water. It was along this that the four marchers made their cautious way.

Legend told Perseus what to search for. Even so, though the instrument looked like an ordinary hunting horn, he hesitated to unhook it from its tree limb. The antler it had been carved from was unfamiliar to any of them.

His companions divided their attention between their young leader and the surface of the lake. Calm it was and calm it remained, but they had no way of knowing what loathsomeness lurking in those depths might soon choose to satisfy its curiosity about the unnaturally animate shapes stalking the shore.

Finally Perseus took down the horn. A single length of black chain fastened it to the branch. The branch had grown round in a spiral so that the chain could not be slipped off.

He touched the mouthpiece to his lips. Nothing happened; he was not struck dead. The mouthpiece was nothing more than a mouthpiece, though extraordinarily cold to the touch.

He took a breath and tried to blow a single clear, unwavering note. The sound that issued from the horn was clear, but broken and discordant, the wail of something rising out of nightmare.

It faded into the fog, lingering eerily. To make certain their call was heard, Perseus forced himself to blow the horn a second time.

Evidence that it had indeed been noted soon materialized out of the mists: the boat was long and narrow, occupied by a single figure clad in black cloak and hood.

"Charon," said Menas softly.

"For once I could do with a surprise," Solon said, and his hand tightened on his sword.

Noticing the reflexive movement, Perseus said urgently, "Hands away from weapons, Solon. We confront no mortal here. You cannot slay the dead."

The boat was as black as its master and boasted a massive figurehead at the prow consisting of the antlers of an elk that had not trod the earth for thousands of years. Castor remarked on their eight-foot spread as they moved toward the slowing craft.

It touched gently against the land. The hooded steersman waited patiently in the stern as the four boarded. No words were spoken.

Perseus exchanged looks with his companions, then steeled himself and walked to the stern. He held out the silver.

The hand that accepted the coins was bare

of flesh, as was the skull that grinned out at him from beneath the black hood.

Keeping his attention on the spectral figure, Perseus moved backward, almost tripping over one of the many benches. The wind whistled through the brush on shore . . . or it might have been a laugh.

Charon turned and leaned on his pole. Effortlessly, he pushed free of the soft mud enfolding the keel. The boat turned about and started out into the lake.

XI

The fog nestled close around the boat and particularly its passengers, but never seemed to touch the ferryman. It would curl around a man's body and then pull sharply away, as though it found the living form unworthy of additional caressing.

Perseus took up a position in the bow, tense and fearful, but at the same time shaking with anticipation. They were entering a realm unknown to the living and visited only briefly by the dead on their way to the underword.

Eventually a rocky beach emerged from the fog. Perseus had tried to mark their course. It seemed as though they'd traveled in a straight line, but with the fog concealing everything it was impossible to be certain.

Several large openings blotched the cliffs that rose from the beach. The boat grounded on the submerged bottom. Perseus looked back, saw the ferryman pointing with a skeletal hand toward the cave directly in front of them.

"Can it know where we wish to go?" Menas whispered.

"Maybe. Maybe all the living who come this way want to go that way," Castor suggested.

Perseus stepped out of the boat. The water was cool on his sandaled feet. "We'll go as he indicates, but slowly. If it seems unpromising or dangerous, we'll try another cave." He turned and leaned back to study the sheer cliffs ringing the beach. "There doesn't seem to be any way inland except through the caves."

The others disembarked. His boat again empty, the ferryman leaned hard on his pole and turned to head back out into the mist in search of another cargo.

It was neither day nor night on that beach: a curious in-between illumination lighted the island. The interior of the cave they cautiously entered was lit from above.

"It leads inward," said Menas, indicating the sandy floor, "and see how it slopes upward as well."

"Better up than down in this place," said Castor with a grunt.

The cave was lined with cut stone, though by what hands they had been shaped and placed none could imagine. Tombs of unbelievable antiquity opened from side passages off of the main tunnel. Their architecture and style suggested use by creatures other than men.

"Remember always," Perseus reminded his companions as they ascended, "that we go to confront a Gorgon. One look from her is enough to finish you.

"If we have to watch her, we must use the inside of our shields like mirrors. That's why I ordered all the leather linings removed. A reflective surface may prove your only salvation. Her mirror image can't harm you, but never look directly at her."

"A difficult way to fight," muttered the nervous Castor. "Backwards."

"Yes," Perseus admitted, "but preferable to being dead. Better than spending eternity here as a piece of sculpture!"

Menas tried to show a confidence he didn't feel. "We're still four against one. No matter how ugly she is, or how dangerous her gaze, she is no warrior." He pulled his sword and swung it backhand. It hissed through the air.

"Four swords and one is enough to kill. We've heard nothing to say that she's invulnerable like the Kraken. For all the tales I've heard, I'm still not sure I believe—"

"You'd best start believing, Menas," Perseus cut in, pointing at the floor just ahead. "Look there."

They hurried forward. Menas put up his sword and began using his hands to move sand. The arm this digging exposed was beautifuly detailed. It was also solid rock, and it ended at the shoulder.

Menas lifted it, passed it over to Solon.

"Not bad," said the soldier, "but I've seen better work in the streets of Corinth."

"You think it a sculpture?" Perseus gasped.

"I didn't say that." Solon sounded defensive. "It's only that we can't be sure of this legend yet. Whoever lives here and passes herself off as 'Medusa' might be an outlaw or banished queen seeking refuge. What safer place than the Isle of the Dead? A few pieces of broken statuary scattered about like this would be enough to frighten off any pursuit bold enough to get this far."

"No farther than that rationalization," said Castor.

"We'll see." Solon dropped the stone arm as Perseus signaled them forward. Together the four headed onward, leaving the arm behind.

"Human?" Menas wondered aloud, gazing back to the resting place of the bodiless limb.

Perseus shrugged. "Who knows?"

We will, and soon, he told himself.

The cave finally opened onto a treeless plain bordered by cliffs. A badly damaged but still imposing temple stood alone at its center. It was as quiet here as it had been on the Styx, though the fog was just a little lighter.

Perseus headed for the building, the others close by. Mist drifted among the thick marble columns and along a wide staircase that fronted the building. As they started upward, the mist began to play about their feet.

Something made a noise on their left. They froze, swords and shields ready, hearts nearly so.

What slithered out from the depths of the temple to momentarily caress the head of a broken statue was unusual only because of its size. The great constrictor ignored them as it slithered down to the ground and off into the fog.

The men relaxed a little. "I've seen them nearly as large in the southern provinces of the Nile," Menas informed them. "Nothing magical about a snake, even one so big. It saw us and ran."

"It did nothing of the sort," Solon countered. "It went its own intended way, and lucky we are not to have been in its path or to have caught it hungry."

"Enough talk of appetites," Castor grumbled at them. "Just now I've none of my own and I don't like this talk of tempting something else's."

The snake did not return and they saw no others as they entered the temple. The ceiling was cracked in places but the columns supporting it looked strong enough. Moss grew in cracks and in places on the marble where water trickled down, indifferent to any sanctity that might have once inhabited this place. Now it was home only to the smell of death.

But the men had long since resolved they

would not be defeated by smells or signs. Solon was climbing another set of stairs when the rock he'd been pulling at suddenly tumbled over and fell past him.

The rock turned out to be a statue of a warrior hunched over in a contorted, unnatural position. The sculpture fell to the floor and shattered, its head bouncing to a stop near Perseus's feet.

He glanced down at it and quickly decided not to call the others over to look. The expression on the statue's face could not do their confidence any good.

They stood listening while the sound of the crash echoed around the temple, eventually fading off into silence.

"That should be enough to wake the dead," muttered Solon.

"It's not the dead we're concerned with," Perseus reminded him. Then his head jerked forward. "Wait—hear that?"

Castor's fingers tightened on the hilt of his sword. "Nothing. . . . no, wait, I hear it. Chains, I think. Someone dragging chains."

Perseus took a cautious step backward. His gaze traveled to the empty spaces overhead. "Watch for nets. This is no place to be trapped."

But the threat was not from above. The rattling gradually grew louder, and from somewhere ahead came a low cough that might have been an incipient growl.

In the darkness ahead and to one side, a pair of eyes suddenly appeared. Almost immediately they were joined by a second pair. The growling was definite now.

Perseus and the others slowly started backing away. The eyes seemed to follow them. They glowed brightly in the darkness, four eerie little lanterns.

The eyes vanished, but the sounds of metal dragging across rock did not. Perseus turned to his right, trying to keep the source of the sound within view.

Then a sudden, concussive roar exploded from one side and he found himself thrown across the floor as something heavy, warm and unyielding slammed into his ribs.

As he rolled over and over on the pavement, fighting to regain his breath and keep from falling on his own sword, he heard a scream. Instantly he was back on his feet, ready to challenge whatever had charged them.

It was restrained by a long chain which allowed it only enough range to cover the staircase they'd been climbing. At first Perseus thought it was a wolf—the largest he'd ever seen.

But there had been four eyes. Were there two of them?

Then the creature moved farther out into the light and revealed itself. The monster was indeed a wolf far larger than a man. But there was only one. It had two heads.

One was snapping and probing at the screaming, frantically twisting body of Menas that it held pinned under a huge foot. Throat-hunting, Perseus knew. Castor lay groaning in pain nearby, one arm laid open by the teeth of the second set of jaws.

Shock faded quickly as Perseus and Solon rushed to Menas's aid. By now the head had hold of the unfortunate soldier's arm and had nearly chewed it through. The other head glared at the approaching men.

"Watch the feet," Perseus yelled at his companion, "as well as the teeth!"

They darted in as close as they dared, staying just out of reach of those snapping jaws. But the wolf-thing was quick and they cut no more than fur. Meanwhile the moans of pain from poor Menas were fading rapidly as the second head made a meal of him.

"Get in closer!" Perseus yelled to his companion. "We've got to get close to it!"

Solon tried, barely throwing himself clear as powerful jaws snapped inches from his neck. The wolf was unexpectedly agile for its great size, and Solon could not distract it long enough for Perseus to strike a solid blow or pull Menas free.

For Menas it no longer mattered. His wounds were massive. But Perseus and Solon had troubled the monster to the point where it was now angry enough to devote its full attention to them.

One head dug deeply into Menas's body. The soldier was unconscious and did not scream. The powerful neck twisted up and over, and the man was thrown high over the wolf's back. There was a distinct crack as the limp form struck the marble floor.

Now the wolf started forward. It was still chained, but they couldn't be sure of the chain's exact length, and a wrong estimate could be fatal.

Perseus tried to move to his left. The wolf cut him off. Both men found themselves being backed steadily up a spiral stone staircase.

"Menas, crawl away now, while it's intent on us!" Solon shouted, dividing his attention between the stalking wolf and his friend below.

"Save your wind, Solon." Perseus swung the sword in a broad arc. The wolf flinched, growling from two throats. "His neck's broken and likely his back too. I heard him hit."

Suddenly it seemed that both heads were momentarily focused on his companion. There was no more time for words, or for thought. He might not get another opening.

He sprang forward, staying low and leading with the sword. It cut completely through the monster's flank.

It let out a horrible yelp and fell backward, taking the sword and Perseus with it. Together they tumbled over the side of the staircase. Perseus fell on something warm and soft. The creature had landed beneath him. Hurriedly he climbed clear and pulled the sword free.

"You've killed it, sir!" Solon was hurrying down the stairs to rejoin him.

But the wolf was far from dead. It had two heads. Now it seemed it might also have two lives. Rolling quickly to its feet, it started backing Perseus toward the near wall.

For the first time, Perseus felt real fear. I ran it clear through and it's not even swaying! he thought in panic. Can it be an immortal thing, immune to a sword stroke?

The wall was very close. Soon he would have nowhere to run and one of those two slavering heads would nip in while he was busy fending off its mate.

He thought furiously, swearing steadily and silently. If I can't kill the thing, at least maybe I can reduce the odds.

He took another step back, then ducked aside instead of backing as jaws snapped like a hunting trap just above his left shoulder. Saliva spattered his face as he rushed forward.

The sword swing was half wild, but the half that remained true cut cleanly. One of the two heads spun free of its neck. Blood spouted from the severed stump and the remaining head howled in pain.

It snapped at the sword when Perseus tried to repeat the maneuver and continued backing him. Perseus tried to slip aside, but there was another wall there. He'd reduced the odds—but at the price of finding himself trapped in a corner.

He tried to stay on the left side of the monster, the side now devoid of danger, while aiming one swing after another at the remaining head. But the monster had learned. It was wary of the sword and took care to avoid every cut Perseus took.

If it trapped him against the wall, Perseus knew it would rush in and overpower him with sheer strength.

Again he ducked, this time feinting at the head with the sword and driving those teeth back. Instead of bringing the sword back for another swing, he changed its arc to a thrust and aimed for the chest, hoping desperately that the monster had a heart. Its blood was red enough.

And it was not immortal. The sword struck true and straight and the monster shivered convulsively. It rose on its heels, towering over Perseus for a moment, before falling backward. This time he didn't withdraw the sword.

It lay on the floor twitching and kicking for several moments. Then it was still.

When he was certain it was dead, Perseus removed the sword and cleaned it on the fur of the carcass. His breath was unsteady and his hands shook a little.

Solon was helping the wounded Castor bind up the vicious slash in his arm, using a strip of material torn from his own cloak.

"A fight for the bards long to sing about," Castor was commenting as Perseus approached. He winced as Solon tightened the bandage. "A fine help I was in it, too."

"You could not have done more," Perseus reassured him. "None of us reacted in time to the beast's first attack. As for songs, no one will sing of us until we are safely out of this place." He indicated the bloody bandage.

"How bad?"

Castor gritted his teeth as he moved the arm. "Ugly, but I've had worse."

"Can you still use it?"

The soldier nodded. "I think so, if I'm careful with it. That thing only opened the forearm. I can still swing. And I've another arm."

"What of Menas?"

"As you thought," Solon told him, "Dead. It's as well that the monster broke his neck. He could not have survived his wounds. The thing had been eating on him before it threw him away."

Perseus turned to gaze into the depths of the temple. "Then it's three to one now." He helped Castor to his feet and they resumed their inspection of the interior.

A half hour of searching revealed nothing save a great quantity of statuary and a maze of empty corridors that invariably dead-ended against the inner temple walls. Nothing else materialized out of the darkness to challenge them. Only the still-bleeding corpse of the wolf-monster remained as a token of the dangers of this place.

"There's nothing here, unless it's too well concealed for our eyes to find," Perseus finally decided. "We've checked the upper balcony and the level we entered on."

"Perhaps there's another below," suggested Solon. "There are so many columns and passages we might easily have overlooked the entrance in this poor light."

"Possible," Castor agreed, still favoring his bandaged arm.

So they resumed the hunt, their attention now directed downward: It was Perseus who eventually found the hoped-for staircase leading into the depths.

"A good guess, Solon," he told his companion.

Castor eyed the hole doubtfully. "Hades lies that way. Remember where we are."

Somehow Solon managed a smile. "Then we'll have to take care not to descend too many steps."

They started down.

Castor's worries were soon alleviated. The staircase ended in an underground grotto forested with marble columns. Whether it comprised the cellar of the temple above or the long-forgotten hallways of a still earlier sanctuary none could say.

One thing was instantly apparent, however. The place was occupied—dozens of torches illuminated the subterranean chamber. Something living required light here.

Whose lair they had entered was also obvious. Everywhere they found the petrified bodies of animals and men. Not even Solon could doubt any longer that it was no sculptor who had fashioned these forms. They were far too detailed, too lifelike for even a master carver to have wrested from bare rock.

Their presence was disconcerting enough, but the variety of contorted expressions on those frozen faces was more horrible still.

A vile sense of humor had been at work among them. One figure would hold out a flickering torch in a frozen hand, while another would brace a damaged column with stone shoulders. They threw distorted shadows on the damp walls. Even Perseus could not keep from throwing an occasional nervous glance over a shoulder to see if the figure just passed might not have moved a trifle.

He kept his shield high and his senses alert. The most difficult thing would be to avoid looking for the source of any sudden sound, especially after the near fatal encounter with the wolf-thing. They would have to battle their natural inclination to use their eyes, and fight with only their ears for guidance.

The grotto narrowed, then opened into a spacious chamber. It ended in an ancient altar backed by mosaic work and a stairway leading upward. A sickly pool of water curved before the altar, the stains bordering the water hinting at unknown rituals and uses.

They started for the stairs, then quickly halted. The faint whisper and crackle of the torches was replaced by a thick, sibilant hiss.

"It comes," Perseus murmured. "Shields."

The three men raised their shields over

their eyes, huddling together for protection against whatever was approaching.

The hissing was directly ahead of them and close by.

"Back away," Perseus ordered his companions, "and don't look. Find a column to hide behind."

They kept their shields before them, fighting down the maddening impulse to look at whatever was near. Each took a turn looking backward to check their path, seeking several columns close together.

Perseus slipped behind one of red marble, now faded and chipped. He hesitated as long as he dared. The hissing was loud in his ears. Then he stepped out from behind the column, his shield held high and his back to the threatening sound.

Despite the horror revealed in the highly polished surface, he managed not to drop the shield.

At the head of the stairway was an enormous snake, cousin in form and body to the great constrictor they'd encountered outside the temple. It was an ichorous green and as thick around as a cedar.

At one end it changed into a scaly sort of degenerated flesh. A human waist began there, a mockery of the beautiful skin that had once been. It varied in places—some smooth, some rough and scaled.

The upper torso was clad in a brief wrap

of opaque cloth and showed the silhouette of a woman. Instead of hair, the head was a knot of writhing, tailess snakes. Perseus had expected that, from the tales he'd heard. What he did not anticipate was the sheer demonic energy in that face.

The teeth were not squared off, but pointed, like the canines of the wolf. Reptilian scales covered the entire face. The eyes—he struggled not to turn and look directly at them—the eyes were a violent emerald green, shockingly bright and piercing. If any humanity had once looked out from them, it had long since vanished.

In her hands Medusa held a heavy war bow. A quiver of hunting arrows were strapped to the leathery back. As he watched, she selected one of the arrows. Instead of notching it in the bowstring, she deliberately touched the point to one forearm and dragged it across the skin.

The scales parted as if at the touch of a razor. The blood that appeared in the wound was almost black. Smoke rose from the incision and the blood bubbled as it contacted the air. Showing no sign of pain from the self-inflicted wound, the Gorgon wiped the tip of the arrow in the smoking blood, then set it to bowstring.

Her gaze is protection enough, he thought frantically, yet she takes no chances.

He would have to turn toward her again. He spun, making certain the shield was well up in front of his face. He raised and lowered it without pattern, taking care to keep his eyes on the floor whenever lowering it below his line of vision.

"Bow and arrow!" he shouted to his companions. "Keep your shields in front of you and vary the height, so she can't set on a target, and get back. She's ready to fire."

"How can we fight her?" asked Solon from one side. "If she's using arrows she'll never let us in close!"

"Back off for now. We'll find a way."

They obeyed, starting backward. Perseus edged round to his left, trying to use the concealing columns to get behind the Gorgon.

Solon followed his instructions carefully, but Castor was still troubled by his wound. With his mind divided between his pain and the Gorgon, he lost his footing as he stumbled through the ritual pool.

His thoughts on keeping his eyes averted from the figure ahead, he turned away. But in so doing, he exposed his back.

The Gorgon let loose the arrow. It struck the retreating soldier squarely in the back. Castor let out a shocked scream of a timbre rarely heard even on the battlefield. He staggered forward, dropping sword and shield as he groped wildly for the burning arrow. It was hissing as the venom burned away the cloth and skin.

Mercifully, he fell face down into the water. The fire from the puncture spread to encompass his whole body. Even the pool began to steam violently.

Despite the horror that was her face, Medusa was capable of a smile of satisfaction. She notched another poisoned missile and prepared to select her next target. Perseus kept darting in and out from behind the columns, but that did not trouble her. The man was quick but she could easily cut him off and dispose of him at her leisure.

She was more concerned about the other, who was already safely past the pool and backing toward the exit. He might escape. She hesitated only a moment before raising the bow.

The arrow shot across the chamber. Unlike the unlucky Castor, Solon held on to both his balance and his wits. The arrow struck the base of the shield and flew off to splinter harmlessly against the ceiling.

The impact, however, knocked the shield out of Solon's hands and sent him tumbling backward. The shield landed on its edge and rolled out of reach, prompting a rasping shriek of delight from the Gorgon.

At that point Solon committed the fatal mistake of looking back to see how close his enemy was.

Those burning green eyes locked onto his own, and he was lost. They held him motionless. He could not tear his eyes away from that mesmerizing stare. And soon it did not matter.

As Perseus watched, his last friend and ally turned slowly gray. Flesh stiffened as a process normally requiring millions of years of heat and pressure occurred in a few seconds.

When it was over, Solon had joined the army of forlorn souls inhabiting the temple, a dead piece of rock empty of life, a caricature of humanity.

Perseus regained his senses barely in time. The next arrow grazed the rim of his shield. Solon's fate had provided Medusa with only momentary pleasure.

As with his lost friend, the force of the arrow sent him tumbling. But unlike the unfortunate Solon, Perseus managed to keep control of his shield. One thing he'd already resolved: he might die pierced and smoking like poor Castor, but he would perish as a creature of flesh and blood, not as a toy forever subject to Medusa's mocking laughter. He would die a man.

Keeping his gaze averted from the monstrosity on the steps he scrambled for better cover behind one of the larger statues.

Medusa was finding this game diverting. She hissed with delight and supplely glided down the stairs. With only one opponent remaining she could afford to relax and toy with him awhile. It was rare that she had the pleasure of live company.

From behind the statue Perseus watched her approach in the mirrored surface of his shield. Mightn't it be used another way? He slipped it off his arm and leaned it carefully against a second statue.

The plethora of torches must mean that Medusa had the vision of a normal creature and could not see in the dark. The flaming brands were in place for her benefit, to expose her enemies to her.

If they must fight, then let her suffer under a handicap too, he thought.

Making a quick dash for yet another of the statues, he swung his sword in a wide arc. It cut cleanly through the torch he'd aimed for. The burning wood tumbled into the ritual pool and sputtered out. A louder hiss came from his stalker but he didn't turn to see where she was.

A moment's pause, then another dash and another torch out. A third, a fourth. The light in the chamber lessened and the shadows grew deeper as darkness began to steal through the grotto.

Medusa started to hunt more seriously among the columns, bow at the ready. The last of her quarry was proving unusually elusive. In the increasing darkness it was hard to tell shadow from man. There— She fired and the arrow just missed the streaking, dodging Perseus, shattering on the wall just behind him.

This was no good. The man must have exceptional hearing. He must be avoiding her by listening for the sounds of stone grinding beneath her body. She stopped and listened

intently herself, eyes flickering like green flame
in the dimness.

Another torch went out and she whirled,
too late to see the man who'd knocked it free of
its holder.

"Medusa!"

Her body whipped around again. The
man's boldness was astonishing. There he was,
gesticulating at her from the base of the staircase, hopping in and out from behind a column.

A fine game, this, she thought. But time to
put an end to it. He was taunting her by
matching his agility against her own. Well, he
was quick, that she wouldn't deny. But not so
quick as an arrow. She permitted herself a
toothy grin. Soon he would be something less
than quick and she could study him at length.

She let the bow and arrow hang loosely, as
though she were indifferent now, but all the
while she was sliding to one side to obtain a
slightly better angle.

Once more he jumped out, making faces at
her. The shield he held before him was broken
along the rim, whether from the force of her
arrows or from being sent flying against the
rock she couldn't tell.

In her excitement at finally having a clear
shot, she failed to notice that the shield Perseus
held was different from the one he'd entered
with.

The arrow was sent flying straight and true

toward its intended target. There was a metallic whang as it hit the man in the chest, instead of the soft thuck it usually made when piercing flesh. The image of the man went flying through the air, a distorted, flattened shape.

For a second the Gorgon was overcome with confusion. It was followed by a hot flash of outrage.

The image!

Tricked!

She'd been stalking the man's reflection in a shield.

Perseus let fly the broken shield he'd found with all his remaining strength. As a youngster he'd participated in all the traditional sports. Though slighter of build than many athletes, his wiry strength enabled him to become fairly competent at such events as the jump, the run . . . and the discus.

The Gorgon was just turning when the serrated edge of the old shield struck her, decapitating her as neatly as an axe. There was a brief, half-begun shriek that was cut off quickly as the head spun from the neck. Perseus had turned away the moment he'd let loose the shield, lest his eyes contact those of the severed head as it fell.

When he finally regained the shield and used it to look toward the thrashing noises filling the chamber, the sight was enough to make him want to vomit.

The headless body of the Gorgon still

writhed and jerked spasmodically with a ghastly, animate life of its own. It curled and tightened about a nearby column. Gradually this sprung watchspring of tortured energy ran down and the muscular snake shape was reduced to a harmless twitching. Blood flowed in a steady stream from the stump of the neck. He would have to hurry.

Using the mirrored inner surface of Castor's shield, he worked his way toward the place where the severed head lay. Removing his cloak, he bent over it and, still keeping his eyes averted, managed to wrap the head in the material. He had to be careful to avoid the dripping blood. Where it touched the floor it ate away the marble.

But it did not seep through the cloth of crimson protected by the power of the crystal eye borrowed from the Stygian Witches.

The floor of the grotto was turning into a steaming inferno as blood from the headless corpse bubbled away the marble and steamed away the waters of the ritual pool. He started to recover his own shield, only to discover that a thick stream of the venomous liquid was flowing between it and his present position. It was wide and shallow, too broad for him to jump. The base of the shield was already dissolving into the corrosive fluid.

A face that had spoken to him once before, in the amphitheater outside Joppa, reappeared now in that dimly lit surface.

"Go now," the voice directed him. *"Tomorrow is the eve of the longest day. Go, and swiftly."*

Perseus needed no additional urging. As the marble continued dissolving, ancient columns began to groan dangerously. The blood was threatening to undermine the entire temple complex. Any second now it might come crashing down on him and all his hopes. He'd not come this far and accomplished this much to lose it all in a simple rockfall.

Holding the precious prize under one arm and his sword in the other, he turned and raced for the staircase.

Behind him, the face in the shield impassively watched his retreat until the metal vanished in the river of blood.

Whether the souls of the many murdered and petrified by Medusa had ever found rest, Perseus had no way of knowing, but at least now their bodies were returned to the earth. Blood lapped at their bases, stone hissed and was vaporized. The ritual pool was now mother to a cloud of crimson steam.

Groans and creaks sounded louder as Perseus emerged from the entrance to the underground grotto and raced down the temple steps. Moments later he was once more outside the temple. The thick fog and desolate terrain of the Isle of the Dead were like the clean sea air of Seriphos compared to the interior of that unholy structure.

As he neared the entrance of the cave

they'd used to reach the temple, the rumblings behind him increased in volume. A loud lingering roar sounded behind him and he glanced back over his shoulder.

Marble dust thickened the sky as the temple roof collapsed. Great columns that had stood for unknown years toppled to the earth like felled trees. Then the walls tumbled inward with a last, echoing crash.

For several moments the dust-laden mist obscured everything. When it finally cleared, only the broad staircase remained, leading up to a pile of rubble. A dull red stain was spreading slowly over the ruin, and blood still seethed and bubbled somewhere inside.

Soon that liquid virulence too would be exhausted, and the lair of Medusa would be only a memory—one that Perseus would carry with him forever.

If he did not hurry though, forever would end sometime tomorrow night, on the coast of Joppa.

He turned and ran down the sandy slope of the tunnel.

XII

The beach they'd landed on was deserted and unchanged. Fog still cloaked the shoreline and tiny wavelets broke on the sand with a muffled splash.

For a terrified moment Perseus felt the real world had deserted him, that it no longer existed. There was no shore across the lake/river, no land to reach. He would swim for days until his strength finally gave out. Then he would sink, only to rise again as Charon plucked him from the waters to convoy him once more back to the Isle of the Dead. There he would enter a different tunnel, one leading to the final, eternal place of rest far below the earth. He would never know the fate of his beloved.

Nonsense! He shook the groundless fear from his thoughts.

Refastening the sword to his belt, he took
a firm grip on the tightly bound bundle (he
could not bear to grip it in his teeth) and
plunged into the tepid water, swimming hard
for the reality he remembered.

His greatest worry now was that he would
become disoriented in the mists and swim in
circles. Even if he'd possessed another piece of
silver, it wouldn't matter. Charon ferried passengers in only one direction.

As Perseus swam he tried not to think of
what might inhabit the waters around him.
Gradually he began to tire; it was a long swim,
even for an experienced swimmer like himself.
Finally, he was almost longing for the sight of
the skeletal boatman and his cargo of dead
souls when his hand unexpectedly encountered
something hard.

Drawing back with a jerk, he almost let
loose of the bundle clutched tightly in his other
hand. Something long and curved leaned toward him through the water.

That's all then, he thought wildly. I'm finished. Medusa's dead body has come searching
for its head

Then the water and the fatigue cleared a
little and he saw that it was only a thick root,
gnarled but not scaly. He slumped in the water, hoping there would be no more surprises.

One hand grasped the familiar shape and
he pulled himself under the arch of the great
root. There were others to be negotiated, but
they grew steadily smaller. His feet touched

bottom. There was no describing the feeling of relief that went through him at that first muddy contact.

Soon he was again on dry land. He lay sprawled on naked rock, his eyes drinking in the sight of bullrushes and water weeds around him. Tantalus's shoulders could not have throbbed worse and his arms were lengths of chain hanging limply down.

He rested for a while, gathering strength. Then he rose and called briskly. No reply. Not even echoes could live on that shore.

Left or right, he mused. It seemed he must have drifted south, but no ... he thought to check the water. The current did indeed push southward. Therefore he should go to his right.

He started off in that direction, still dripping wet since there was no sunshine to dry him, shivering from more than just cold.

There was no dramatic reunion when he finally stumbled back into the camp: Thallo and Philo were seated by a fire, wondering about the possibility of a storm, and Perseus simply stepped through the reeds into the clearing.

Thallo rose immediately and walked over to greet him. The two men stared at each other for a long moment. Then Thallo looked past the exhausted Perseus, hesitated, finally looked back into the younger man's face.

Perseus shook his head slowly.

"All of them?" Philo looked up from beside the fire.

"Medusa." Perseus walked over to the old tree which overhung the clearing and searched through the supplies stacked there. Finding the length of rope he wanted, he used it to secure the damp bundle to a branch. It swung gently in the rising breeze. Then he returned and collapsed next to the fire, drying himself and gnawing on a piece of dried meat as he spoke.

"She won't kill any more good people," he said tightly. "Her temple's destroyed . . . I thought I'd never make shore . . . and the temple's guardian with it. A monster wolf-dog with two heads that we had to kill before we found her. It killed Menas."

"Dioskilos," murmured Thallo. "I've heard legends of such. And you slew it as well as the Gorgon?"

Perseus nodded. "Almost lost Castor to it as well." His voice dropped. "As it turned out, it didn't matter."

"Three good soldiers." Thallo turned back, looked out across the reeds. "Three good men."

"Good friends," added the disconsolate Philo. He nodded toward the bundle tied to the tree. "You gained what you came for?"

"Yes. It still bleeds. Don't touch it."

"No worry of that," said Philo fervently.

A rumble of thunder reached down from above and lightning made the fog glow like a lamp. Thallo put hands on hips and gazed skyward.

"Curse these mists. I cannot tell if it will rain or not."

"Zeus is angry," said Philo, "about something." He was setting up the small bronze pot in which they would cook their supper.

"Zeus is always angry about something." Thallo spat to one side and moved to check on the horses. They stood quietly nearby. "Prince, perhaps we should try to make some distance toward home before nightfall."

Perseus shook his head and tried to smile. "You would have to tie me to the horse, my friend. I have no more strength." Something whirred at him from the top of a rock bordering the nearby stream.

"Yes, my mechanical friend, I know that flesh is weak and metal strong, but I still wouldn't trade with you."

Bubo hooted once, eyes flashing, and settled back to study the landscape.

"You'll feel better after a night's sleep and some real food," Thallo assured the younger man. "If we leave before daybreak we can still make Joppa in the time left to us. Even Hercules had to rest from his labors."

"He couldn't have been more tired than I am." Perseus found a blanket and wrapped it around his still damp body. In minutes, he was sound asleep.

Philo stirred the contents of the bronze pot. "Should we wake him for supper?"

"Nay," Thallo said, studying the silent figure in the blanket. "He needs rest now more than food. We'll feed him in the morning."

Thunder sometimes disturbed the peace of the night, but it didn't wake the men. By first light they still slept on, oblivious to Zeus's complaints. Bubo rested on his rock, ticking away somnolently.

The red bundle swayed gently in the wind. Nearby the water reeds rustled uncomfortably in the rising breeze. Or perhaps they moved because of the muscular figure that walked cautiously among them.

Calibos had seen Perseus's return to camp. He'd spent this night waiting patiently, as he had for several days. There had been no need to interfere. He was confident Medusa would finish his work for him.

Now it was clear she had not, and he would have to finish himself what the Gorgon ought to have done. His repeated entreaties to Mother Thetis had been met with silence as he'd followed the expedition out from Joppa.

When they'd separated back by the lair of the Stygian Witches, he'd been sorely tempted to kill the old man riding with the princess and carry her back to his lair. But that would only have angered Thetis, who had pronounced final judgment.

In his thirst for revenge he'd inadvertently goaded the goddess into demanding the death of the one love he could not command. Now that the princess's death was ordered, all he could do was insure that her lover did not survive her.

Perseus lay huddled by the ashes of the dying fire. Somehow the cursed man-child had fooled the old witches into helping him and had slain Medusa.

Well, he would not find Calibos so easy an opponent, and he would pay him back now for the loss of his hand.

Moving as quietly as possible, Calibos made his way behind the tree holding the scarlet bundle. Once, the braided whip coiled over his shoulder caught on a projecting branch and he almost cursed aloud before freeing it.

As he leaned around the trunk of the tree, he used the trident fastened to the stump of his left forearm to brace himself. It was a poor substitute for a hand, but the best he could contrive.

With a sharp knife he cut a small gash across the bottom of the bundle. The stink that wafted from within assured him that the Gorgon's head had not yet dried out completely.

No amount of kicks or blows of the whip had been able to compel his swamp servants to make the long march with him. Under no circumstances would they journey beyond the marshlands. He could not hope to defeat three experienced warriors, however, without assistance.

He permitted himself a slight smile. Perseus was brave and lucky, but he lacked knowledge. Calibos knew all the legends, all the details of the great mysteries. How ironic that the ignorant Perseus should thus provide Calibos with the means of his destruction.

Yes, there was still a little blood left in the severed head. A few drops fell from the slit fabric to the ground while thunder railed impotently above.

The mitigating atmosphere of the Isle of the Dead was not present here on the soil of the real world. If the legends were correct . . . yes, the earth where the blood had dripped was beginning to seethe.

Soon the suppurating soil coaxed forth all manner of wriggling vileness: blood-engorged leeches, swollen maggots, worms with black skin, and tiny agitated scorpions. Of them all, only the fiercest and most lethal would survive to draw on the power of Medusa's blood.

Backing away, he hid himself behind the tree.

Quickly, the worms returned to the earth. The leeches melted and the maggots became food for those who remained. Three scorpions began to grow.

Calibos watched with interest and delight. Another few minutes and it would be too late for the sleeping travelers. He shifted to the other side of the tree in order to have a better view of the end, and thereby stepped on one of the few dry dead twigs in that fog-shrouded land. It cracked like pottery.

It was a modest noise, most likely lost in the rush of wind and occasional lightning. But it was heard by one whose ears were far more sensitive than those of men.

Bubo was suddenly alert. His head clicked around to focus on the three arachnids. His eyes spun and flashed as he generated a hoot of alarming dimensions, a mighty clanging the likes of which are not heard outside the metal foundries of Luxor.

Thallo and Philo came awake instantly and reached for their swords. Perseus was only seconds behind them.

"Damn you, you unnatural meddler of metal!" Calibos stepped out from behind the tree and uncoiled his whip. Bubo continued to rail away. "You won't interfere again!"

The whip shot out and snapped violently against the figure clinging to the rock. Bubo was spun off his perch, wings flapping furiously but tardily. Still sounding his alarm, he landed in the stream. His raucous ringing blended into the sound of rising bubbles as he sank.

"Nothing will save you this time, Calibos," said Perseus, fully awake now. "Not the vermin who serve you, not your immortal half-mother: nothing."

"It's not I who need saving, bastard. Or have you not looked to your prize?"

The three men turned, and froze. The three scorpions were now the size of ponies. They ignored the half concealed Calibos and advanced toward the larger cluster of food. The food drew together and readied for the attack.

"Watch the tails," muttered Thallo, keeping his eyes on the advancing creatures. "They'll hold enough poison to kill instantly."

"Poison be damned," said Philo. "Those stingers are as big as swords."

"Easy, easy," Perseus urged his friends, his own sword waiting. "Try to separate them, take them one per man. That way they can't surprise us from behind."

One scorpion was slightly closer than the others. It snatched at Perseus with a huge claw. He stepped nimbly aside, fended off a strike of that looming tail, and swung his sword. It cut a piece of chiton from one claw and the scorpion jerked back in pain.

"Now," he yelled, "split them up!"

Swinging their swords like scythes, Thallo and Philo joined Perseus in the charge. The three scorpions were forced apart, leaving each man with only one opponent to worry about.

"I'd enjoy watching," Calibos called pleasantly, "but I've other work to do. Do me the pleasure of waiting for my return." He turned away and limped off through the reeds.

Thallo could hear the sound of the whip cracking behind them. "The horses!" he yelled. "He's driving off the horses!" He ducked and weaved just in time to avoid another strike from a deadly tail.

There was nothing they could do about their mounts. The monsters continued to press in. Though the three men held them off, none could gain an advantage.

Enough time wasted on this, thought Calibos finally. I will alter the odds.

He stepped into the clearing and selected a target. The whip spun, became a noose around Philo's neck. Putting his weight into it, Calibos yanked hard. Philo went backwards to the ground.

Immediately the scorpion he'd been battling rushed in. The tail hooked and went clear through Philo's body. He screamed and tried to twist free as Calibos methodically drew back his whip.

Perseus saw what had happened and deliberately stepped close to his own attacker. As the expected pincer reached for him, he cut down. The limb dropped to the earth as the tail descended. That too was severed. Before the monster could back away, Perseus rammed his sword through its head. It buckled like a broken cart.

Meanwhile Thallo had dealt with equal success with his own enemy, gradually cutting off bits and pieces of it until it had little left to fight with. He drove home the final blow as something dark and thin tightened around his neck and pulled him backward.

"Thallo!" Perseus rushed toward him, but found himself intercepted by the scorpion which had killed Philo. Desperately he hacked at it as he watched Thallo being pulled inexorably toward the reeds.

The old soldier was strong, but the whip choked away his breath. He continued stumbling, his hands trying to pull away the whip, until he impaled himself on the three-pronged weapon which occupied the stump of Calibos's left arm. His eyes widened.

Calibos withdrew the trident and let Thallo's body slump to the ground. His gaze lifted to Perseus cutting apart the last of Medusa's seed.

He started toward him. It was nearly finished, he mused happily. Let Thetis pronounce her curse; he would fashion his own revenge. He had the trident and the whip. He would make this last death a lingering one.

One more thrust finished the scorpion. Perseus pulled the sword clear just in time to ready himself for a more conventional attacker. As he turned the whip snaked around his sword arm and pulled.

Perseus went down and the sword fell from his grasp. He managed to fight free of the whip, reached for the sword, but something bit into his neck and he went over backwards, twisting in pain.

"Come on, boy. I've only one hand to fight you with, as well you should recall. Surely you can defeat a tired, ugly, one-handed man. Or even a one-handed beast such as myself." When Perseus did not move, Calibos's tone grew threatening.

"Come, get up. There's only you left and no one to help you. There's your sword, so close." He cracked the whip at it, sent it skittering across the ground. "Why don't you pick it up? Then you can cut off my other hand and win yourself another bride with it—your first is doomed."

Perseus clenched his teeth and ignored the taunts. His only concern now was how to regain control of his sword. But every time he tried to rise or move toward it, a hot, searing agony shot through his body and sent him to the ground.

"Get up, Perseus," Calibos chided him, setting the whip again. "It's only a little whip. Horses take it better than you—even hogs. Don't let it keep you down in the slime with the worms, lest you think you belong there."

Though he tried his best to ignore the pain, Perseus could get no closer than a couple of feet to the sword. Whenever he drew near, the whip would wrap around his ankle or leg and drag him back through the mud.

He rested a moment there, allowing Calibos to tease him. Then he made as if to rise again and reach for the sword. Out of the corner of his eye he watched the whip arm move and tensed in expectation of its strike. As expected, it snapped around his right ankle.

The fire shot through him once more, but as the whip was receding he lunged for it. Before Calibos could pull it clear, Perseus had it wrapped around his arm. Now he dug his feet into the earth and started pulling toward the sword.

Calibos leaned back, trying to keep Perseus away from the sword while regaining control of the whip. The youth's legs were knotted with muscle, so that despite the other's greater weight, Perseus was dragging him inch by inch toward the blade.

With a frustrated cry of blind rage, Calibos let the whip handle go and charged. The trident hand was raised high to strike the final blow.

But the sudden release of tension sent Perseus tumbling . . . straight toward the sword. He knew he could not hope to fend off the fresher, heavier Calibos while lying on the ground, and his arm trembled with the strain as he turned onto his back and heaved the weapon with both hands.

Calibos stopped about four feet away from Perseus. He stood there, staring down at the panting, whip-scarred youth. Slowly the trident hand came down as both hands clutched at his middle: the hilt of the sword pressed tight against his skin; the point and several inches of blade emerged from his naked back.

He turned away from the prone form of Perseus, bumped up against the tree, staggered several steps to one side, and then keeled over. He made no noise when he struck the ground, and he did not move again.

Perseus lay breathing hard, unable to move. Eventually he rolled over, got to his knees, then his feet. This exhausted him all over again and he nearly fell. His tunic was in rags. Blood streaked his exposed flesh, marking the places where the whip had cut deep.

His first thought was for his companions. He'd seen the scorpion's tail pierce and kill Philo. Old Thallo was dead also, lying on his back staring blankly at the sky, his expression a mixture of surprise and outrage. After decades on the battlefield, he'd finally been felled by a cowardly blow from behind.

Perseus limped to his side, kneeling with an effort that made him dizzy. On the second try he was able to close those staring eyes.

"Sleep well, old friend." His voice shook. "A truer friend no man ever had."

He stood, but there was no strength in his limbs. He crossed to the tree and took down the cloaked head of Medusa. The slit in the bottom was dry now. There was no more blood in the head to work further mischief with the innocent earth.

Turning, he started across the stream. One foot caught and sent him tumbling into the shallow water. Joppa . . . have to return to Joppa, he thought desperately. Horse or no horse.

He let himself drift across the gentle stream, crawled out on the far sandy bank. He still held the bundled head of the Gorgon.

It was as far as he could go, and not nearly far enough to save the princess.

XIII

The fog had lifted a little and the sun penetrated enough to warm the sand, the newts and lizards that foraged by the water's edge, and the body that slept with its feet still trailing in the stream.

Perseus's eyes opened slowly. He didn't know how long he'd lain there asleep on the bank, but a strange sound had brought him out of his lethargy.

There it came again, grinding and yet somehow kind to the ear.

His head lifted and he looked down at the water.

A line of small bubbles was moving steadily toward the bank. A silvery reflection appeared on the surface, emerged as a feathery dome.

The owl moved stiffly until it was standing

next to the youth. Shaking metal wings he sent water flying into Perseus's face. The cool droplets helped to revive him.

Bubo gave forth several waterlogged hoots and clicks while Perseus listened intently, delighted to see his little friend once more.

"Hello again, my damp counselor. Yes, we've both spent better nights." He winced as he rubbed his cramped legs. "I can understand your confusion. I don't see too well underwater myself. I thought we'd lost you for good." Bubo responded with a succession of agitated clicks.

Perseus managed a smile. "You shouldn't apologize for walking in circles all night. Owls are supposed to have good sense of direction, but not underwater. The important thing is that you finally found your way out. But I'm afraid all may be lost." He gestured to the other side of the stream, toward the reeds and rushes that masked the carnage of the previous night.

"Calibos will trouble us no longer, but I fear he'll have his revenge anyway. He drove off our horses. They must be halfway to Joppa by now, if not slain by some beast. It doesn't matter. I haven't the time to try to hunt them down.

"Thallo and Philo are dead." He paused, his throat dry, then looked across at the little owl. "That means it's you and me, my little friend." Bubo hooted softly, sounding as hopeful as metal could.

"Calibos is dead too, but I'd rather fight him than Father Time. If you can still fly, and if he still lives, you must try to find and bring back Pegasus. He's our only hope now."

Querulous hootings.

"I don't know where he is. He didn't meet us at the Wells of the Moon. I can't believe he turned completely wild again.

"Try to the north and east of the Wells, and in the marsh where Calibos was lord. He knew enough to follow us this far. Maybe he also knew enough to interfere with Pegasus. Fly to him wherever he is, little shadow of the night, and bring him to me, else I'll stay here to die. At least my journey to the underworld will be a short one, and fate may place Andromeda and me in the same boat."

Bubo let out a shrill whistle. He flapped his wings experimentally, turned and tried to take off. Water squirted from sockets and joints, but that slowed him only temporarily. More than mere muscles gave him the power of flight.

He started down the stream bank, flapping furiously and hopping along on little pistoning legs. He bounced once, twice, and it seemed for a moment that he would end up ingloriously in the water again. There was no third bounce.

He skimmed low over the stream, avoided a snapping fish, and gained altitude. High overhead, he circled once and dipped his wings in farewell.

Perseus waved, then watched the brilliant spot of light until it vanished southward. At that point he lay down on his back on the warm sand and allowed himself to lapse into a second sleep.

Once the skull had been that of a beautiful mare. Now it served only to support the torch which threw uneven light across the interior of the cavern.

The marsh throne was empty, awaiting the return of a lord who would never sit on it again. Calibos's principal servitor, the gaunt huntsman, stood lazily by a large wooden cage. He was rebinding the head of his spear. Inside the cage Pegasus paced nervously.

The vulture which perched close by was partly the cause of the stallion's anxiety. The lumbering carrion-eater was quiescent now, looming motionlessly over cage and huntsman like a section of sculpted rock. The great hooked beak was red with the blood of fresh death.

The huntsman frowned as he worked on his spear. Lord Calibos had been gone unexpectedly long from the marsh. The huntsman hoped he returned within the fortnight. If not, then the huntsman was charged with slaying the wonderful flying horse, a task he did not relish.

He tied a last knot and walked toward the throne. The spearpoint needed some final sharpening.

He was setting it against the whetstone balanced there when an alien sound caused him to glance up. The vast red eyes of the vulture opened abruptly, and in the cage Pegasus pricked up his ears.

Nothing was visible outside the cavern entrance save the mists. With a grunt, the huntsman returned to his work.

Something small and unnaturally fast came whizzing into the cave. It circled once round the roof of the cavern as the astonished huntsman looked on. The vulture shifted nervously on its perch.

The metal apparition suddenly changed course. In the enclosed air of the cave it sounded like a gigantic wasp. Talons spread, it dove straight for the huntsman.

That poor worthy threw up his hands to shield his face and let out a startled cry. Bubo passed just above him, rustling his hair. It was enough. Waving his hands protectively above his head, the creature forgot Calibos and his orders and fled from the lair.

Calibos's remaining servant was larger but as easily startled. Bubo turned in midair and rushed heedlessly at the huge vulture.

Without intelligent direction the enormous bird was helpless. It yelped and hopped down from its perch. The beak snapped ponderously at the tiny clicking, whistling shape which was tormenting it. The massive beak could have turned Bubo to scrap, but it never came close.

Pursued by a hooting, wheezing nightmare that had no scent, the vulture flapped its wings and began retreating. One wing knocked over several of the torches. The lair was carpeted with rotting vegetation and dry organic matter. In a matter of minutes it was filling with flame. Pegasus kicked at the bars of the cage, his eyes rolling wildly at the fire.

With a last measured peck Bubo forced the vulture from the cave. Behind him sounded the neighs of the frantic stallion as the flames licked steadily closer to its cage.

Bubo turned. It took him only seconds to solve the problem. Using his beak, he pulled on the rope trip which held the counterweight. The weight dropped and the door shot upward. Pegasus immediately dashed out into the cave, followed closely by Bubo.

They were on their way out into the open when the marsh gas which filled the lair suddenly ignited in an explosion that rattled the whole mountain.

In contrast to the violent eruptions that shook the marshlands, distant Joppa was silent as a tomb. The marketplaces were quiet, devoid of their usual frenetic activity. No captains filled the air above the docks with angry curses and cries, no slaves unloaded cotton from Aegypt or marble from Greece. All of Joppa was deep in mourning for a death which had not yet occurred.

In the palace Cassiopeia stared in frozen

silence as her only child emerged from the sanctified pool in which she'd been given a final cleansing. This horrible parody of the marriage eve was forced on her by the conditions of Thetis's curse. Half a dozen ladies-in-waiting commenced to dress the princess.

How pale she is, Cassiopeia thought. Much paler than normal. As I no doubt am. But I must try not to let it show. The people back me, look to me to save them. I cannot let them down.

I will not let Andromeda down. See how bravely she bears up under the terrible strain. It would not do for her own mother to break down while she maintains such dignity and calm. Characteristics she takes from me, along with her physical beauty and quick mind. Characteristics she will never be able to enjoy or use in the service of her people. Characteristics doomed to uselessness by the capricious whim of an outraged goddess.

Thetis, she cried silently, why could you not punish me instead? But she knew the goddess was doing precisely that.

There was nothing to do but finish it.

A solemn crowd had assembled in the square outside the palace. Today there was no division between soldier and priest, merchant and citizen. All were joined together in common despair.

Their feelings were augmented by the slow, steady beat of the drummers flanking the palace entrance. There was very little conver-

sation. All knew what had to take place today;
all knew that Andromeda was to sacrifice herself to save the city. Dozens of women had
volunteered to take the princess's place—futile
gestures, for Thetis's demand had been specific.
But it made Cassiopeia feel better.

A little.

She dropped the veil and by herself placed
the farewell coronet of flowers on her daughter's head. Mother and daughter gazed into
each other's eyes. They shared the same lin-
eage, the same blood, and each knew her place
and obligations.

No tears clouded Andromeda's eyes. For
now, at least, she held back the fear. If Perseus
had not come, it meant he had failed. If he had
failed, then he must be dead. And if he was
dead, she had no desire to live.

The procession left the palace. There was
none of the usual cheering when the royal party appeared, only a murmur of sympathy from
the crowd. Soldiers were not needed to make a
path, the crowd parted silently.

Ammon joined the procession there, silently doing his best to comfort the queen. They
made their way down the palace steps. Citizens
leaned silently from windows and trees to
watch the procession pass, and threw garlands
of olive and laurel leaves in its path. Only the
soft lament of the drums broke the quiet.

Even the city gates seemed unnaturally
muffled when they were swung open. Soldiers

and priests led the column out of the city, turning south along a well-worn wagon track.

The cliffs that sheltered the southern part of Joppa's harbor rose high and straight from the water. It was a favorite play-place of children and fishermen.

In ancient times the barbarians who had lived where Joppa now flourished used to perform their rituals by a particular rock which jutted out into a cliff-shielded cove. A path led down from the crest of the cliffs to the old place of sacrifice. No children scampered along it today.

All were children, though, to others who watched them assemble along the rim. Zeus stood and stared into the image centered in the amphitheater of life, brooding and silent.

Hera, Athene, Aphrodite, Poseidon and Thetis were grouped around him. His silence was sometimes as dangerous as his quick temper, but Thetis, having committed herself and her prestige as a goddess, was not to be denied. She stepped up to him and spoke resolutely.

"Great Zeus, on Earth it is now the eve of the longest day. You have agreed to uphold the laws by which we immortals exist. Do so."

"I like not this business," the king of the gods muttered. "The game has gone too far."

"Law demands what you do now. Your own law."

"I know, I know." He turned from the

amphitheater, his voice full of bitterness. "It must be. Release the Kraken."

Poseidon bowed slightly. "As my brother commands." There was just a hint of sarcasm in his voice, but Zeus was too upset to take note of it. He turned and left the chamber.

Zeus returned his attention to the scene in the amphitheater. Behind his back his fingers locked and curled, their movement as intricate and troubled as his thoughts. Somehow it had all gotten out of hand.

The procession was filling the peninsula which jutted out into the cove. Four priests flanked Andromeda, who was followed by Cassiopeia, Ammon, and the ladies-in-waiting. It was close to sunset. They would have just enough time to comply with Thetis's demand.

Soldiers and citizens who'd straggled along in the wake of the official procession now spread out along the edge of the drop. The rock of sacrifice waited below, a basalt finger pointing away from the city—a pleasant place on most days, haunted only by the forgotten memories of less civilized times.

The black-clad priests had assembled their massive calling horns. These were usually used to bring the people to prayer, or to announce festive occasions. Today they would sound a dirge.

Chains and manacles had been readied on the sacrificial rock, for despite Andromeda's acceptance of her fate, there was fear among the priests that the sight of the Kraken might cause even one so strong-willed as the princess to forget her vows and try to flee. Andromeda had not argued with their proposals, had accepted their embarrassed suggestions as calmly as she had everything else.

Now her mother, the old playwright and the ladies of the court stood back while the priests gently helped the princess down the steep path. They were determined that she would not suffer so much as a scratch during the descent. Let the vengeance of the gods take its awful course, but good servitors that they were, they would keep her from harm until the last possible moment.

One priest had tears in his eyes. An older companion chastised him sternly.

"Do not weep and shame us before the princess, who does honor to us all."

Until now it seemed that calm would prevail, but for all her resolve and inner strength, at the last, Andromeda was no more than young, human, and terribly frightened. As the first manacle locked tight around her right wrist her overstrained nerves finally gave out. She started struggling and screaming like any mortal.

More shocking still to the onlookers was the sudden, piercing shriek that came from higher up, from the queen. It was the first time in twenty years of rule that anyone had heard the queen lose control. Ammon tried his best to quiet her, but the controlled resignation that had governed the royal party so well was breaking down all around him. The other ladies of the court, including the personal servants of the princess, set up an unceasing wailing.

"Quickly," said the high priest through clenched teeth, trying not to look at Andromeda's pleading face. "Secure her and let us be away from this place." He could feel his own will cracking under those pitiful sobs.

At last it was done: the four manacles were locked, and she was fastened to the cold rock. The priests hurried to climb the path, unable to keep from brushing at the dirt they felt but did not show. None of them would forget the last screams of the princess no matter how long they served the city of Joppa.

The dying sun neared the western horizon. The day was almost done. On the cliffs the great curved horns commenced their languorous baying, acknowledging the end of a day which would go down in the archives as the saddest in the history of the city.

The sun reddened the waters, a portent of what was to come. Horrified and yet unable to move away, the assembled citizenry waited with their priests and queen to see the fate of their doomed princess.

Finally a young girl pointed and a murmur of unrest rose from the crowd. To the southwest the sea was beginning to boil, foaming with a force that hinted at something enormous below.

There was a great roar of displaced water as that immensity erupted from the depths. Screams and shrieks of terror came from the crowd, which instinctively pulled back from the edge of the cliffs. Then the waters subsided. For a time nothing was visible in the water save a great towering fin which was moving steadily toward the little cove.

Andromeda was barely conscious, her screams having faded into a steady whimpering. She kept her eyes averted from the cove and tried to tell herself it would soon be over.

A vast wave crested against the rocks ringing the cove, as a great sucker-laden tentacle lifted into the air and wrapped itself around a rock the size of the palace. Its mate surfaced soon after and sought a grip on the other side of the entrance to the little harbor. Then the rest of the massive body pulled itself above the water.

The head was covered with scales and spiny growths, a huge beak overlapped the mouth. The dragonesque tail switched in the water and sent waves smashing against the rocks. Eyes the size of ships glared down into the cove, shining with a restrained fury barely held in check by a treaty thousands of years old.

The last of the Titans gazed at the people lining the cliff and yearned for release from that binding. But it knew its limits; today only one miserable life was to come to it. The power of the gods still constrained it. Poor as it might be, however, a death was still a death.

As it turned its attention down toward a certain rock and the small life that still throbbed there, its head buzzed with a peculiar droning. Suddenly a small flying thing oɪ metal shot across the frozen landscape of its face.

Bubo fought to distract the Titan and just avoided the sweep of a massive tentacle. The wind of that immense limb's passing was enough to send the owl spinning. It tried to regain control, failed, and spun into the rocks. There was a nasty, sharp clang. The owl did not shatter, but neither did it rise again into the sky.

The Kraken's gaze turned once more to Andromeda. Much as the Titan might have wished her single death to linger, the day was almost gone and it was under order to finish the simple work by dark.

If the one life was not present in the designated place, the Titan had been promised an entire city to destroy. But the life was there, and in its frustration at having so little work to do, the immortal was anxious to finish it quickly and return to its lair beneath the sea. There it would brood in silence, awaiting a more rewarding day.

The life below was twisting and writhing frantically, a small thing to engage the attention of so vast an instrument of destruction. The Kraken was used to battling gods and whole armies, not a single helpless mortal. Nevertheless, compulsion demanded.

A great tentacle began to descend. Andromeda turned her face to the rock and waited for the end.

Wings sounded in the sky again, and again the Kraken paused. The little metal thing which had irritated it was a motionless lump on the rocks. This, it decided, was a different sound.

Diving down out of a sunset sky came a cloud. On its back rode a scratched and bruised figure of muscle and determination. It wore no armor, carried neither sword or shield. Instead, it held tightly to a wad of red cloth.

There rose no cheer from the assembled citizens. Already this eve they'd witnessed two manifestations of the gods. A third left them struck dumb.

They watched in awestruck silence as Perseus and Pegasus swept low overhead, but a tingle of excitement, of hope, was beginning to rise in some.

The Kraken slid slightly backward in the water, uncertain what to make of this second and much larger aerial intruder, but ready to swat it from the sky as quickly as it had the first.

Perseus dug his thighs hard into the stallion's flanks. Using his legs to steer with, he directed Pegasus toward the head of the Kraken, now looming below like the crest of a mountain. With his hands Perseus began to unwrap the tangled bundle he carried. The rushing wind made it difficult to handle, a difficulty compounded by the fact that he dare not look too closely at his burden.

Cassiopeia hardly dared allow herself hope as she followed the path of man and horse through the sky. For one of the few times in his life old Ammon could not find appropriate words.

By now Andromeda too had noticed the arrival of her betrothed. She was too emotionally drained to do more than stare.

Perseus had planned well, but as so often happens, the best of planning is upset by the most mundane details. He'd decided in advance how to approach the Kraken, what angle of descent to adopt, when to flash the head of Medusa. All he had overlooked were the stubborn knots he'd tied in his cloak. Now he was wrestling frantically with them.

Too close, too near! He dug hard at the stallion's flank with his right leg. Pegasus swerved, almost too late. A tentacle the width of a river slashed at them. It barely nudged the horse's hindquarters, but the blow was enough to send him tumbling off-balance seaward.

Desperately the stallion tried to right itself, but there wasn't enough air space between it and the water. It rolled once, twice, and Perseus was thrown clear. Still clutching the red bundle, he fell head over heels. The impact of striking the water broke his grip. Pegasus plunged into the sea nearby.

Only an outstanding swimmer could have survived that impact. Perseus flailed at the water and fought his way back to the surface. Still sore all over from the concussion, he floated there, fighting to replenish his breath.

Hindered by its own bulk the Kraken turned slowly, hunting for the man who'd fallen from the flying horse. Perseus dove and swam for the nearest rock. There was no sign of the precious bundle.

It had slipped away from him when he'd struck the water. Now it was rising from the sea next to him, rising in the gleaming talons of a hesitantly clicking Bubo.

By one of those ironic coincidences that fate seems so fond of, the rock nearest Perseus was the one that projected farthest into the water. So in addition to finding himself again on dry land, Perseus also discovered he was momentarily reunited with his love.

He staggered out of the roiling waters in front of her and their eyes met for an instant. That was enough to sustain him throughout eternity, he knew. He whirled to face the Kraken, which had located him again. Perhaps, he thought with grim satisfaction, love will give him indigestion.

At which moment of final despair, Bubo swooped by and dropped the still-bound cloak into Perseus's waiting hands.

The owl rose and soared close by the Kraken's eyes. It was enough to distract it for a few precious seconds. Without having to worry now about maintaining his seat on the flying horse or fighting the wind, Perseus unknotted the cloak. He reached in, warning Andromeda to keep her eyes averted, and grasped a handful of cold, rubbery coils. Pulling it clear of the cloth, he held out the face of Medusa to the Kraken.

Freed of the bundle's artificial night, the eyes of the Gorgon opened. The snakes Perseus gripped grew agitated. He held fast, ignoring their cold caress as they wiggled between his fingers.

The Kraken, last of the Titans, was stopped still in the water, mesmerized by the still sublimely evil power of the Gorgon. The huge inhuman eyes began to cloud over. Slowly the great tentacles slumped, the dragon fins stiffened. While those on the cliffs looked on in amazement, the immortal turned to stone.

That massive body was thousands of years old. It could not survive alteration of shape or consistency. Once petrified, the Titan began to crumble. Huge chunks avalanched from its sides.

As it exfoliated it became unbalanced. With a final, irrevocable rumble that signified the passage of an eon, the shell of the last Titan tumbled slowly backward into the open sea.

When the wave this threw up had subsided, Andromeda risked opening her eyes, still careful to keep them away from her love and the abomination that had saved them. "Is it over then, Perseus? Are we truly safe at last?"

"Almost," he said grimly. Drawing back his arm, he heaved the loathesome relic as far as he could.

It landed in the cove, and there was such an eruption of foam and steam where it landed, one would have thought Hades itself had risen to take lasting possession of it.

Eventually the hissing died down, the bloodred waters dispersed, and the cove was once again nothing more than a pleasant place for children and fishermen to pass the time.

The manacles and chains were impossible for the imprisoned to reach, but simple enough for a free person to unlatch, especially if he was as determined and eager as Perseus. In moments the princess stood safe and free in his arms while a vast sigh of relief and wonder rose from the assembled multitude.

There came a last, awful moment as the sea resumed its boiling. But there was only the one Kraken. What sprang from the water as though propelled by a catapult was not a threat, but the revived Pegasus.

It climbed rapidly, seeming to have to find its wings all over again, like a butterfly emerging from a watery cocoon. The people oohed and ahhed in delight, while Cassiopeia and Ammon hurried down the path to rejoin the reunited lovers.

Pegasus whinnied forlornly for his friend and Perseus responded with a shout. There was little room on its chosen rock to stand and the stallion moved to another. It stood there, trying to keep its footing, while the foolish bipeds nearby made human-noises at each other and engaged in a lot of mutual patting.

How silly a way to spend one's time, the horse thought in its own fashion, when there are so many beautiful things to taste. It cropped at the wild flowers growing from the rocks.

Once more the temple of Joppa was filled with celebrants, and again the decorations of life garnished the walls and columns. There was an unfinished ceremony deserving completion, and the entire population of Joppa tried to crowd its way into the temple to witness that consumation.

The words were spoken as they had been so many days ago while the elders in the crowd watched and nodded with satisfaction.

The old poet too looked on from his place of honor among the wedding party. A metal owl perched next to him, proud despite its dents and bruises. This time the ceremony was not interrupted by a voice from behind, for the statue of Thetis no longer dominated the temple ... or the lives of those assembled inside it.

Cassiopeia spoke the final words. Her hands moved rapidly, almost defiantly as she tied the silken ribbon around the youngsters' wrists.

Nothing stopped her. It was a day of triumph for men.

Perseus and Andromeda turned and embraced while the people shook the temple to its foundations with their cheers.

Among them were a few equally happy but less demonstrative.

"You know, my badly dented little friend," Ammon said confidentially to Bubo, "this would make a fine heroic poem. Or perhaps even a play."

A nervous chirping issued from the owl, which even Ammon thought he could understand.

"Oh, don't worry, guardian of the night. I won't leave you out."

Bubo expressed his pleasure, though to Ammon it sounded more like a waterwheel coming apart.

Two of the hundreds present were oblivious to the sounds of celebration and to the byplay between man and machine. They finally separated, but not far. Perseus glanced up at the ruins of the once magnificent statue of Thetis. His expression was visible only to a few.

There were additional small rituals to carry out. The sooner they were concluded the better he would like it. He turned and led Andromeda down the stairs and away from the impotent marble.

"Perseus has won." Zeus smiled, looking up from the amphitheater where the symbols of life were fading from sight. "My son has triumphed."

"So it seems." Hera gave him a cool smile. "A most fortunate young man."

But Zeus was not about to have his pleasure diluted. "Fortune is ally to the brave and clever. He defeated the Kraken. He defied the powers of Thetis. He dared to face the might of the gods and win!"

"Courageous, handsome and intelligent. A true hero," murmured Aphrodite admiringly.

"And you keep away from him," said Zeus warningly. "These young lovers need no further interference from the gods, especially from one as overpowering as yourself."

Aphrodite turned demurely aside. "I am hardly overpowering, great Zeus. Merely persuasive."

"Keep your persuasions away from Joppa."

"It is a dangerous precedent," declared the frustrated Thetis. "What if one day, others like him should arise? Humans ready to defy the gods and go their own way?"

"A good question that, my husband," agreed Hera. "What if courage and imagination became everyday mortal qualities? What would become of us?"

"No more sacrifices, no more belief, no more need to depend on us for guidance," Zeus replied without concern. "We would no longer be needed. Mankind would learn to deal with the universe by himself.

"You worry too much, my dear. For the moment, at least, there is sufficient cowardice, sloth, and mendacity rampant on Earth to last for some time." He looked up from the distant reaches of eternity where he'd been searching and his tone changed to one of warning.

"I forbid any further attempts at revenge against Perseus or those close to him. He has done well, better than many gods might have done." There were outraged whispers from the other immortals.

"And he shall be rewarded, as shall those who believed in him."

Andromeda lay with the man who loved her. It was a night of spectacular clarity, but there was more mystery and wonder in his eyes than in the heavens.

Had she looked outside, she might have seen a subtle glow in the night sky. Nothing had truly changed, but a new awareness of certain patterns had been injected into the minds of men. As of that night and time, certain groupings of stars came to be forever identified with the participants of those memorable events.

There a cluster of stars seemed now to take on the outline of a bold young man, though the stars had always been there. It was mankind's awareness of them that was altered.

Another distant pattern assumed the silhouette of a young woman, and still another that of a winged horse, and yet a fourth an older but still radiant lady.

"Let the stars be named after them forever," Zeus declared from high Olympus. "Perseus the brave, Andromeda the true; the noble Pegasus and even the vain but caring Cassiopeia.

"As long as man walks the Earth and looks questioningly into the night sky in wonder, he will remember the courage of Perseus. For *ever,* even if we gods are abandoned and forgotten, for the stars will never fade. And mankind will look on them and remember. Until the end of time. ..."